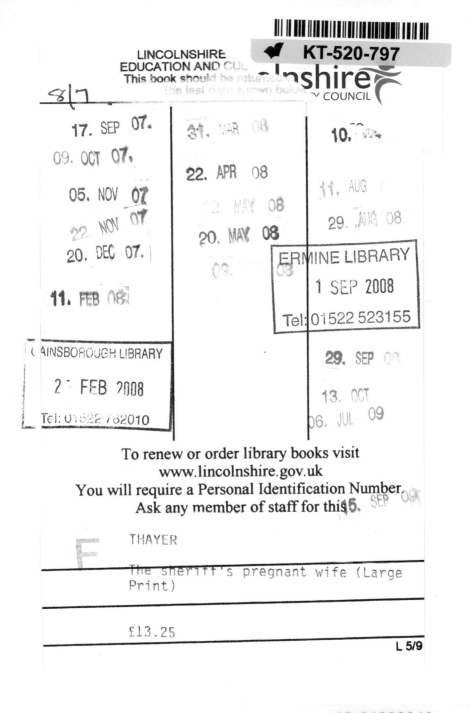

To renew or order library books visit
www.lincolnshire.gov.uk
You will require a Personal Identification Number.
Ask any member of staff for this. 15. SEP 09

THAYER

The sheriff's pregnant wife (Large
Print)

£13.25

L 5/9

THE SHERIFF'S
PREGNANT WIFE

THE SHERIFF'S PREGNANT WIFE

BY

PATRICIA THAYER

MILLS & BOON

Pure reading pleasure

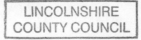
All the characters in this book have no existence
outside the imagination of the author, and have
no relation whatsoever to anyone bearing the same
name or names. They are not even distantly inspired
by any individual known or unknown to the author,
and all the incidents are pure invention.

First published in Great Britain 2007
Large Print edition 2007
Harlequin Mills & Boon Limited,
Eton House, 18-24 Paradise Road,
Richmond, Surrey TW9 1SR

ISBN: 978 0 263 19483 8

Set in Times Roman 17½ on 21 pt.
16-0907-40162

Printed and bound in Great Britain
by Antony Rowe Ltd, Chippenham, Wiltshire

CHAPTER ONE

P<small>AIGE</small> K<small>EENAN</small> needed to make a career change. And soon.

She could no longer live in Denver, not with a chance of running into…her past. Pushing aside the bad thoughts, she peered in the window of the empty brick storefront with the For Rent sign.

Although the light was dim, she could see hardwood floors, and ornate door moldings and trim that was characteristic of a 1916 building.

Intrigued, she tried the large brass knob. Surprisingly it turned and she pushed open the solid oak door.

"Hello," she called and her voice echoed

back. "Is anyone here?" Stepping into the long, narrow room, she looked around. All at once she could picture the space as hers. A reception area adorned with oriental rugs and ferns and farther back a divider, separating the space for her private office.

Her excitement increased as she continued her search. It had always been her dream to one day have her own practice, but she'd gotten sidetracked with the excitement of working for the D.A. Suddenly her vision seemed to be more of a possibility—no, a necessity for survival.

Could moving back to Destiny be the answer to her situation?

In the back of the space, Paige found a storage room and another door. She tugged on the brass knob and it opened to a staircase. When she flipped the switch, a single light went on overhead, and she climbed creaking steps to a large musty-smelling room. Scarred hardwood covered the floors, and a tiny kitchen was tucked in the corner. Chipped cabinets hung open, displaying leftover canned goods from the last tenant. She was drawn to a bank of windows and a long, built-in bench beneath them. On the opposite wall another door led to a bedroom and small bathroom. Everything needed a good cleaning, and some paint.

She returned to the main room. It would take a lot of work, but she could make this livable. A shadow fell over the already dim room and through the windows she noticed dark clouds blocking the sun from the small Colorado mountain town. The wind picked up and it began to rain. Lightning flashed across the sky and seconds later the crash of thunder followed.

Paige turned to leave and noticed a man standing in the shadows of the staircase. She let out a gasp and her heart pounded in her chest. Another flash across the sky illuminated the gun he was holding.

"Sheriff," he announced. "Stay where you are."

Paige felt the blood drain from her face as he stepped into the light wearing a khaki shirt and a silver badge. Then a familiar face came into view.

"Reed…" she whispered weakly. She tried to smile, but suddenly everything went spinning and her body began to crumple.

Reed Larkin holstered his gun and rushed to the woman just in time to catch her in his arms.

Not just any woman, but Paige Keenan.

Gently he lowered her to the floor, cradling her in his arms. Her silky brown hair fell away from her flawless, but pale face. He placed his fingers against her neck to find her racing pulse.

"Great job, man, you nearly scared her to death. Paige…" He cupped her cheek. The softness of her skin was nearly his undoing. He knew under her lids were those whiskey-colored eyes that had haunted his dreams for years. His gaze moved to her oval face—the straight nose lightly dusted with freckles, the tiny cleft in her chin. A beautiful package. His attention rested on her full mouth as he recalled how she had tasted…

It had been nearly ten years since he'd last seen her, but he'd never been able to shake the feelings she evoked in him. His pulse went into overdrive, his palms began to sweat. Damn, it was like high school all over again.

"Paige, wake up. Come on, honey. Let me see those big beautiful eyes."

Finally she shifted, making a soft moaning sound, and murmured the words, "My baby." Her hand moved across her stomach.

Paige was pregnant? Reed glanced at her ringless finger. She wasn't married. Before he had the chance to react to the news, her eyelids fluttered open.

"Reed…"

"Hi, Paige," he managed to say. "I've always dreamed of women falling for me, but not like this." He smiled, but quickly grew serious. "How do you feel? Should I call the paramedics?"

"No! I'm feeling better." She sat up slowly, avoiding his gaze. "I just forgot to eat…and you scared me to death pointing a gun at me."

"You are trespassing."

"The building is for rent and, I might add, the door was unlocked. I only came inside to look around."

"We've had some kids vandalizing." He frowned. Was Paige moving back to Destiny? "Are you looking for office space?"

She climbed to her feet and brushed her hand on her nicely fitting jeans. "Maybe. Any problems with that?"

He shrugged. Problems? *Only about a dozen.* "Just surprised that a big-time Denver attorney wants to open an office in a small town. I thought you outgrew Destiny, Colorado."

Paige straightened slowly, testing her steadiness. What business was it of his now? At one time they'd been friends—more than friends. That was a long time ago.

"I could say the same thing about you. A hotshot FBI agent returns home and becomes a small town sheriff."

Paige gave him a bold once-over. Reed Larkin was definitely more filled out at thirty than he'd been at seventeen. She examined his developed chest and broad shoulders. One thing hadn't changed, he still had deep set bedroom eyes, a strong jaw and black wavy hair. He looked pretty good in uniform, too. But then he'd always looked good to her.

His voice broke into her thoughts. "I had my reasons for returning."

Years ago, Reed swore he'd never come back to Destiny. Never listen to another bad word about his family. Now Paige remembered why he'd returned.

"I heard about your mother's stroke. I'm sorry. How is she doing?" Sally Larkin had once worked at the Keenan Inn. That had been how Reed and Paige's friendship began.

"She has her good days, and her bad ones."

"Is she allowed visitors?"

He nodded. "Your mother goes out all the time."

"Is it all right if I visit her?"

"She'd like to see you." He studied her. "So are you going to be hanging around a while?"

"At least until Leah's wedding."

He nodded. "Holt's a nice guy. They seem happy."

Too bad Reed didn't seem happy to see her. That bothered her. Over the years, she'd missed their closeness. The way they had always been able to share things. That ended when she'd made a decision…to push him out of her life.

If she decided to come back to Destiny, she would see Reed…all the time. That shouldn't bother her, but it did.

Right now, she needed her entire focus on one thing. Her baby. Everything else she would deal with later, including Reed Larkin. So she had to ignore the feelings he stirred in her, blaming it on her already jumbled emotions.

"I should get going," she said. "I'm meeting with Morgan."

Reed raised an eyebrow. "You mean, the honorable mayor?"

"And your boss."

"Oh, I'm shaking in my boots."

His attitude was back and suddenly she was remembering too much…the skinny little boy she befriended when some third-grade kids were picking on him on the playground. But later she hadn't been able to protect him against the sadness over his father's desertion.

"I really should go," she told him, not wanting to return to the bad memories. She turned to leave.

"Paige…"

She stopped at the top of the steps. "What?"

"Have you told your family about…" His gaze went to her flat stomach. "Your condition?"

Paige tensed. How did he know? "I don't know what you're talking about," she denied.

"You murmured the words, my baby," he told her.

She started to deny it, but he would learn the truth soon enough. Everyone would. "I don't want to talk about this now."

He studied her for a few heartbeats. "There was a time we shared…a lot."

She didn't want to discuss her private business with a man who hadn't been a part of her life for years. "No, I haven't discussed it with anyone…yet."

"What about the father?"

Now, she was angry. "And I'm not having this conversation with you, Reed." She waved her hand. "Would you please forget that you even saw me today?"

She swung around to make her grand exit when another wave of dizziness overtook her, causing her to sway.

Reed rushed to her. "Whoa, I've got you." His strong arms went around her back and he guided her down on the top step. "I'm going to take you to the clinic."

She was very aware of the brush of his arm in the narrow space. It seemed to add to her instability. "No, I'm fine."

He cursed. "Like hell you are." He got up and went to the sink and pulled a white handkerchief from his pocket. He wet it under the faucet, then returned to her. He placed it against the back of her neck.

For the past two years and four months, Paige had worked tirelessly for the Denver D.A.'s office where she'd tried numerous criminal cases. But returning home to Destiny had her more nervous than prosecuting a high-profile drug dealer. And Reed Larkin was one of the main reasons. The other was telling her family about her pregnancy.

"I bet you didn't have much breakfast, either."

"My stomach is just a little queasy to eat much, but I was going to have lunch with Morgan," she fibbed, holding the cool cloth against her skin. It felt good.

"I'll call her," Reed suggested.

"No! I'm fine, and I can make it across town square to City Hall. So you can stop playing hero."

He stiffened. "Someone has to rescue you

from yourself." He stood and headed for the door.

Just like ten years ago, Reed Larkin was walking away from her once again. The pain of his leaving this time, surprisingly affected her a lot. She felt just as alone. But just as before, she had to let him go…

Reed berated himself all the way back to the office. He should have just helped Paige out and not asked any questions, and he wouldn't have learned she was pregnant with another man's child.

Most guys had that special girl in high school, the one that was out of their league. Paige Keenan had been that girl to him. Pretty, smart and nice to everyone, but she'd dated the popular boys in school, and he was far from popular. Yet, she had been his friend.

The poor kid from the wrong side of town was off-limits. The boy whose father was the impractical dreamer, always looking for the pot of gold. Michael Larkin used to work the mine, had even partnered in one of his own, "Mick's Dream." Then one day the man walked out on his wife, Sally, a son, Reed, and daughter, Jodi, and never returned.

And no one had seen or heard from Mick in over seventeen years.

Sally Larkin had to take two jobs just to support her children. Later, Reed helped with part-time jobs, but his mother insisted he stay in high school. After graduation, he'd been offered a scholarship back east. His biggest supporter for going on to higher education had been Paige. He resisted a lot, but it hadn't been until she admitted that she'd outgrown their relationship that he had been hell-bent on leaving her and the town. After college, he went to work for the FBI, mainly so he could search for Mick.

Reed had always suspected that his father's

partner, Billy Hutchinson, had something to do with his disappearance. But who was to question the richest man in town. Even with the technology available at the Bureau, Reed still hadn't found any answers, or his father.

Reed had finally put it to rest after a series of things changed his life. The first had been when his partner was killed in the line of duty. He, too, had been wounded, and after his recovery he had gone back to work for the Bureau, but it was never the same.

Then when his mother had a stroke twenty months ago it was the deciding factor. He returned to Destiny. She'd had to go into a convalescent home, and he made the choice to stay in town. For good.

He took a job as deputy, then just last year when the sheriff retired the small community voted him into the position. He had an area to protect, and just two deputies and a daytime dispatcher.

He was making a life here in Destiny. Even though his sister, Jodi, lived in Durango with her son, Nicolas, she was able to come on weekends. He visited his mother nearly every day.

Yes, he was dealing with things…and now, Paige had shown up. For years, he'd managed to keep her out of his thoughts. He now knew as soon as he'd set eyes on her again, it would be impossible to keep her out of his heart.

"Reed Larkin pointed his gun at you?" Morgan gasped as she sank into her chair.

Paige swallowed a bite of her sandwich. She was hungry and the food was actually helping her queasy stomach. "In all fairness to him, I was trespassing."

Her older sister brushed back her long auburn curls. "And what were you doing in the old Merlin building?"

Paige had arrived home last night, just in

time to attend her younger sister's, Leah's, engagement party. She had been grateful that all the attention had been on the happy couple, and she hadn't had to answer a lot of questions. Questions about her career, her future.

She wasn't sure that she wanted everyone to know about her plans…yet. "Can you keep a secret?"

Her sister's green eyes sparkled. "Do you want to pinky swear, or would my word as mayor be good enough?"

Paige laughed. She had missed the interaction with her sisters so much. "Your word is good enough. I'm taking a leave of absence from my job. I'm rethinking my career goals."

Morgan brought her sandwich to her mouth and paused. "Does that mean you're thinking about coming home?"

Paige's thoughts turned to Reed. She'd be living in the same town with a man who's welcome had been on the chilly side. So what! This wasn't high school. He would just have to deal with it.

"Yes, but please, don't say anything to Mom and Dad just yet. I have to consider if I can make a living here." She couldn't seem to come out with the words, *I'm thirteen weeks pregnant.*

Morgan still looked skeptical. "What about your work with the D.A.?"

Paige sighed. "I need a change." And preferably to be far away from her baby's father. Drew McCarran had made it clear that he wanted no part of her in his life. She should be happy about that since all he'd said since they met had been lies.

She forced a smile. "Maybe I'll open my own law practice. What do you think?"

"It's a great idea." Morgan jumped out of her chair and came around the desk to pull Paige into her arms.

"Oh, Paige, this is wonderful. First, Leah returns home and finds the love of her life.

Now, you're back to open your own practice. Leah will be so excited."

The phone rang and Morgan reached to answer it. Paige went to the large window overlooking the town square. There was a comfort seeing the three-tiered fountain where birds fluttered around cascading water. A white lattice-covered gazebo brought memories of band concerts on warm summer nights.

As one of the Keenans' three adopted daughters, Paige and her sisters, Morgan and Leah, had been blessed with charmed lives. Everyone in town had embraced the two toddlers and one infant who'd been left with Tim and Claire Keenan twenty-seven years ago.

Destiny's citizens would be thrilled that Paige was returning home. But what would they think of her when they discovered she'd made mistakes, and now, she had to deal with the consequences.

Morgan walked up beside her. "Sorry about that."

"Well, you are the mayor."

They both broke into laughter.

It was Paige who sobered and said, "Why don't we keep this between you and me? With the wedding in two weeks, I don't want any attention taken from the bride." And the news of the baby definitely would do that. "No matter what I decide, I have a month's leave to investigate my options."

Morgan nodded. "You're right. We need to concentrate on Leah's wedding."

Two weeks. Paige had a two-week reprieve. Her thoughts turned to Reed. Could he put his feelings aside, and keep her secret that long?

Later that evening, the Inn's kitchen was buzzing with activity while Claire Keenan prepared the family meal. Paige's mouth watered when her mother pulled the large rump roast trimmed with red potatoes and carrots from the oven. Claire was easily the best cook in town, and Morgan ran a close second. Even Leah had learned a few things, but Paige was a lost cause in the culinary department. But since her appetite had recently increased with her pregnancy, she'd decided she better learn how to feed herself.

"Would you mind setting the table?" her mother asked as she added flour to the old cast-iron skillet to begin making brown gravy.

Paige's stomach growled. "Sure. Anything to hurry things along. I'm starved."

Her mother raised an eyebrow. "Good. You need to eat. You're too thin."

Not for long, Paige thought. How would her mother take the news about the baby? She walked back to the cabinets, knowing she had to tell the family and soon. She released a breath. Just not tonight.

Her mother looked away from her task, her

gray-blue eyes full of concern. "Are you all right, Paige?"

Paige carried the stack of plates to the large, round table. "I'm fine, Mom. Maybe a little tired. I've just finished a difficult case," she told her. She wasn't exactly lying. She had finished a big drug case. And she ended her relationship with her baby's father.

"Well, your father and I are glad you finally took some time off." Claire smiled. "And we plan to spoil you while you're home."

Her mother's words brought tears to Paige's eyes. She worked swiftly to set the big, round maple table, then looked out through the large kitchen window to the setting sun. Large pine trees lined the back of the property, where a half dozen cabins had been built along a rocky creek.

Paige had loved growing up here. Any kid would. She didn't remember much before she and her sisters had become part of the Keenan family, but she knew she couldn't have had a better childhood, or more loving parents.

Now, with her baby on the way, Paige had questions about her own birth. About where she'd come from. Why had her biological mother left her three daughters on a stranger's doorstep? Maybe it was time to get some answers.

Paige's father walked into the kitchen. "It smells great in here," he said with a big grin and his dark eyes twinkled. But then she'd never known the big, burly Irishman not to be ready with a smile, a hug and a kiss.

"You say that every time you smell food," Claire said.

Tim Keenan came up behind his wife of nearly forty years, wrapped his arms around her and murmured in her ear. Claire blushed, and looked up at him with such unbridled love that Paige had to glance away.

The two had always acted like this. Paige

had taken their relationship for granted. Now, she realized how special it was. Paige envied them. She'd worked harder on her career as a lawyer than on a personal life. Then she'd met Drew. Life had been perfect for a time, then everything came crashing down around her. When she needed him the most he wanted her gone from his life.

The pain Drew had caused her would never compare to the heartache she'd experienced when Reed left all those years ago.

It was an all-too-familiar story.

Back then she and Reed Larkin were friends and it had developed into a crush by the time they'd reached high school. All the girls had been attracted to the rough around the edges guy. Paige knew his tough act had been a shield.

Since Reed's mother had worked at the Inn, Paige had developed a friendship with him. That was until graduation day and they'd both had decisions to make. Paige had always been college bound and then on to law school.

Reed had opportunity for college, too. To leave Destiny and the stigma of his father behind him. But he was willing to turn down a full scholarship to go with her. Not that she hadn't cared for him, just the opposite, but she'd wanted him to have a chance. In the process of convincing him to go away to school, she had to lie, causing her to lose the man she loved…and her best friend.

The familiar ache tightened in her chest as the memories flooded her head. She quickly pushed them away and continued to lay out the flatware. She had to stop reminiscing about the past. The future was what was important now. All her focus should be on her baby.

Men were off-limits.

Reed lived in Destiny, but that didn't mean they had to keep running into each other. It wasn't as if they moved in the same social circles. Her only concern was that he keep her secret for now.

The sound of voices caused Paige to turn around. Her sisters, Morgan and Leah, came through the door. Her baby sister's brown eyes were brimming with happiness, and why not? Leah was engaged to a great guy. She and Holt would be married soon, and they were adopting an eight-year-old boy, Corey. A complete family.

"Sorry, we're late," Leah said. "But we were busy trying to finish up some wedding plans." She took both her sisters' hands. "I need a maid of honor, and I couldn't choose between the two of you."

"It's okay, Leah…" Paige began to say Morgan could have the honor when her sister's grip tightened.

"Just hear me out," she said. "Holt and I talked it over. The only fair thing to do was draw a name. I mean, we'll all be getting married someday, anyway. So we can all take turns. The name I picked was yours, Paige."

Tears flooded Paige's eyes. "Oh, Leah, I wouldn't have been hurt if you chose Morgan…"

"Stop it, Paige." Leah smiled through her own tears. "Remember you don't want to upset the bride-to-be. So just say yes."

She glanced at Morgan. She smiled and nodded. "I'd be honored to be your maid of honor, Leah."

A tall, good-looking rancher, Holt Rawlins, walked to his bride-to-be and hugged her. His sandy colored hair had been recently cut, leaving a soft wave over his forehead. He had an easy smile and green eyes that sparkled with mischief.

"Boy, am I glad that's over," he said. "I'm also glad that I didn't have so much trouble choosing my best man."

"Who's doing the honors?" Paige asked.

"Holt asked me."

Everyone turned to see Reed Larkin standing in the doorway. He was dressed in jeans and a pale blue, Western-cut shirt, and looked devilishly handsome.

"Isn't it great?" Leah gushed. "Reed is going to be escorting you down the aisle, and you two get to toast us at the reception."

"Yes, that's great," Paige agreed as she caught the smile on Reed's face.

So much for not running into each other.

CHAPTER TWO

AFTER dinner, Paige made her way out to the porch. With all the wedding talk it was getting a little stifling inside the kitchen. She also hated the fact that she was keeping a secret from her family. An important, life-changing secret. Even though she'd come home several times since moving to Denver, tonight seemed different. Soon a lot of things were going to be different.

Leah was getting married in a matter of days. Paige was going to have a baby. The Keenan family was growing. In a few months the clan would have added three new members.

She pressed her hand against her stomach

protectively, a habit she'd acquired since learning of her pregnancy. This wasn't the way her mother and father had expected to welcome their grandchild. It hadn't been how Paige planned, either. She'd planned to bring her special guy home this summer to meet her parents.

How could she've been so wrong about a person? She'd believed him when he said he was divorced—that he hated his wife, Sandy.

The day Paige had learned about her pregnancy, Drew announced that he was going back to his wife. In truth they'd only been separated for the past year, and Drew finally admitted that he wanted a second chance at his marriage. What she hadn't expected was his anger and his threat not to get in the way of his reconciliation. Then he stormed out of her condo and her life.

Paige wiped a tear from her cheek, refusing to cry over the man, or the past any longer. It was all about the future. The Keenans were going to be her baby's family. She and her child didn't need any man, especially a man who didn't want them.

"Would you mind some company?"

Paige tensed and glanced over her shoulder to see Reed. She shrugged. "It's a free world."

"Thanks," he told her, nodding toward the back door. "There's way too much talk about Gerber daisies and banana cream or strawberry filling for the wedding cake going on inside."

She raised an eyebrow. "Can't take it? And you're supposed to be the stronger sex."

He cocked a thumb toward the kitchen. "If you think I'm in bad shape, you should see how blurry-eyed Holt is."

That made Paige smile. Although she didn't know the groom well, she liked him. "Losing testosterone, huh?"

"Be careful, I'm feeling the urge to spit and find a belching contest." Reed walked to the railing, sat down.

"I'd appreciate it if you'd resist."

"I'll try." He leaned against the post and looked out at the rows of moonlit pines. "This is nice."

Paige wanted to ignore the fact that his nearness bothered her. What was wrong with her? She'd left those feelings back in high school. "I know. I've missed this place."

Reed turned to Paige. He could see that she'd been crying. He knew from his sister's pregnancy that women got emotional. Paige coming home to tell her family about her baby had to be rough. "Your family is going to be happy about the baby."

She glared at him. "I don't want to talk about this. And you promised that you weren't going to say anything…"

He raised a hand. "Hey, you have to know

I wouldn't break a promise to you. I'm just trying to be a friend, Paige."

She remained silent.

He changed the subject. "Have you seen a doctor?"

She nodded. "Just to verify that I'm pregnant and to start my vitamins."

"You need a doctor here?"

She hugged herself. "I want an obstetrician."

"My sister had a good doctor. She's in Durango."

She nodded, but looked sad.

"Are you sure that you don't want to contact the father…?"

"That's the last thing I want," Paige whispered as she stared out into the night. Reed felt the familiar ache of wanting to take her in his arms and tell her he was here for her.

Damn, he hated that she could still turn him inside out. She'd come back to town and all he wanted was to be with her.

"I'm sorry...that things didn't work out for you, Paige." As much as he wished it, he couldn't make this right for her. Reed looked over at her and instantly wanted her. He always had, but it wouldn't work for either of them. They were both carrying too much baggage.

He stood up. "I should be going. I work tonight." He started to walk away, then stopped. "If you need to get a hold of me for anything, just call the station. If I'm not there, leave a message on my voice mail."

Paige turned around. "Reed, this isn't a good idea...I need to stand on my own. I have a lot to figure out."

He smiled as he reached out and tucked a strand of hair behind her ear, grazing her incredibly soft cheek. "I know, I was just thinking that if you needed a friend."

Her lower lip quivered. "We tried that once."

"Yeah, we did. Maybe this time we can handle it better."

He turned and walked away, knowing he was lying through his teeth. When it came to Paige Keenan, friendship wasn't all he had in mind.

The next morning, Paige woke up about eight o'clock, and made it into the bathroom before she got sick to her stomach. Luckily the family had gone downstairs and she was alone. How would she explain puking her guts out?

Paige showered and dressed in a pair of worn jeans, but had to leave the top button undone. While she put on a pale pink blouse she was unable to stop thinking about Reed. It would be such a bad idea to get involved with him, especially in her condition.

She was vulnerable, and could so easily lean on Reed. And that wouldn't be fair to either of them, even though he had suggested they could be friends again.

Paige smiled. In grammar school she could

be friends with him, but now, the man was too good-looking and sexy not to stir her hormones. Any woman's hormones. No, she needed to stay as clear of Sheriff Reed Larkin as possible. Of course until the wedding was over, that wouldn't be easy.

She arrived in the kitchen to find her mother.

"Good morning," Claire said and kissed her daughter on the cheek. "How about some breakfast?"

No way. "Maybe some toast and juice."

Her mother put a cup of coffee in front of her. Of course Paige couldn't have caffeine during her pregnancy. "I think I'll pass on the coffee. I'm trying to cut back."

"Good. Your job is so stressful that you don't need it."

Paige took her place at the table and her mother brought the toast over and sat across from her. "So what are your plans for today?" Claire asked.

"Nothing until this afternoon when we go shopping for our bridesmaids' dresses. Until then I could help you here at the Inn."

Her mother patted her hand. "You're not here to work. You need this vacation."

"I don't mind," Paige said, needing something to fill her time.

"I have an idea," her mother said. "I'm going out to the nursing home to see Sally. You could come along."

Visit Reed's mother? That wasn't a way to stay uninvolved. "Sure." Paige finished with her toast and cleared away the dishes.

The Shady Haven Convalescent Home was about twenty minutes outside of Destiny. It was a fairly new facility with manicured grounds and the mountains as a backdrop. With its brick trim and red cedar singles the two-story building didn't look like a nursing home, but more like a retreat.

Paige doubted that Sally Larkin could afford

this place on her own. Reed had to be paying a lot of the bill.

Claire and Paige walked though the double doors and notice the inside was just as impressive as the outside. A reception area was arranged around a fireplace, and gleaming hardwood floors. In an adjoining room, Paige could see several patients in wheelchairs, sitting at tables, playing cards and other board games.

Her mother approached the front desk. "We're here to see Sally Larkin."

An older woman with short gray hair smiled. "It's good to see you, Mrs. Keenan. Sally looks forward to your visits." She turned to Paige. "Is this one of your daughters?"

Claire nodded. "Yes, this is Paige. She's visiting for a few weeks."

"Hello, Paige. I'm Karen. I guess you could call me the social director around here."

"It's nice to meet you," Paige told her. "You have a lovely facility."

"Thank you. Our first concern is our residents." She stood and came around the desk, then motioned for them to follow her down a wide corridor. "Sally finished her physical therapy about an hour ago. She's doing very well. And she doesn't have anything scheduled until after lunch, so this is a perfect time for a visit."

They passed several rooms on the main floor. Most doors were open, revealing accommodations that looked more like mini apartments than hospital rooms. There was nothing generic about this nursing home.

At the end of the hall, Karen knocked on a door, then opened it. "Sally, you have some visitors," Karen said as she opened the door wider to reveal a small woman sitting in a wheelchair.

Sally Larkin wasn't as old as Claire Keenan,

but the hard years, and a debilitating stroke had taken a toll. When she saw Claire and Paige, Sally's eyes lit up bringing back memories of the last time Paige seen Sally. Hers and Reed's graduation day.

Paige touched her hand. "You remember me, Sally?"

"Y…yes…" Tears formed in Sally's eyes.

"I hope you don't mind me just showing up."

The woman squeezed Paige's hand. "Wel…come." She struggled with the word. "P…Paige."

"Thank you, Sally. It's so good to see you." She hugged the frail woman, then looked into those eyes that reminded her so much of her son's. "I'm glad you're feeling better."

Claire joined the conversation. "Sally has improved a lot in the past year. She's talking again." Her mother smiled. "I'm glad my friend is back and we can share things. We're hoping she'll be able to come to Leah's wedding."

Due to the stroke, Sally's smile was crooked, but she was obviously pleased. "Doc...doctor said o...okay."

"That's great news," Claire said and looked at her daughter. "The facility has special vans and attendants that can take her where she wants to go."

"Who's taking who where?"

All three women turned to the door and found Reed. He was dressed in a pair of faded jeans and a burgundy polo shirt.

"Hi, Reed," Claire said and went to him. "The doctor said your mother can come to Leah's wedding. Isn't that great?"

He grinned. "Yes, it's great." He crossed the room and kissed his mother's cheek. "Maybe we should get you a new dress."

Sally frowned and shook her head.

"Oh, Sally, you shouldn't turn him down," Paige said.

Her eyes locked with Reed's, and once

again, she was transported back in time to when they were sixteen. He'd driven her to Durango to look for a dress for the prom. She was going with another boy. That had been when he confessed about his feelings for her. He wanted more than friendship.

"We should go," Claire said, breaking through her reverie. "We need to meet Leah for wedding shopping."

Paige patted Sally's hand. "It was good to see you again, Sally."

"C…come back."

"I will." Paige smiled, then looked at Reed to see he was pleased she'd come, too. She walked out of the room and he followed her.

"Paige, thank you for coming by today. Mom loved it. I appreciated it, too."

"It was no trouble at all."

His gaze refused to release its hold. "How are you feeling?"

Her mother had already reached the reception area and was out of earshot. "Better. This morning was a little rough. But I'm good now," Paige said.

He stuffed his hands into his jeans' pockets. "You look terrific."

A shiver went through her. She didn't want to analyze her reaction to the compliment. "I should go."

"Oh, I got the name of the doctor." He pulled a card out of his pocket. "Kimberly York. Jodi said she's the best."

Paige glanced down the hall again to make sure her mother was out of earshot. The business card actually belonged to Reed with his private phone number. The doctor's number was written on the back. "Thank you," she said. "I'll call and make an appointment."

"If you need someone to drive you let me know."

His offer was so thoughtful she suddenly

had the urge to cry. She had to leave. "Thank you, again. I better go."

When she made her way to the reception area, she found her mother talking with a thin man seated in a wheelchair. He was bent over, with sparse white hair that stood out around his head. His face was weathered and lined with age. She blinked and studied the man closely. It had to be…old Billy Hutchinson.

Memories came flooding back to her. All the trouble he'd caused the Larkin family. And worse. Billy's manipulation had change the course of her and Reed's life. It was wrong, no matter if the cause had been a good one. But most of all, she'd always regret the lie…and losing Reed.

She approached them. "Mother…"

Claire turned and smiled. "There you are. Billy, you remember my middle daughter, Paige. She works in Denver now. She's a lawyer."

Paige swallowed her nervousness. It had been a long time since she'd seen or talked to this man. She wasn't eager to now. "Hello, Mr. Hutchinson."

"Bah, lawyers…they're all crooks. Give 'em a chance, they steal ya blind." He peered at her. "Why, you're that gal who hung around with that Larkin boy."

Paige's heart pounded. "That was a long time ago."

"Everything was a long time ago." He waved a crippled finger at her. "You should stay away from those Larkins. They're no good."

After all this time Paige didn't want to rehash this, especially not with Reed just down the hall.

"You shouldn't upset yourself, Billy," her mother said. "That's all in the past."

Abruptly the man's agitation turned to sadness. "No, we can't change the past." His hazel eyes filled with tears. "Can't change a dang thing…what's done is done." He slumped deeper into his chair. "I didn't mean to…" He looked pleadingly at Paige. "It was an accident."

"What accident?" Paige asked.

He choked on the next word. "Mick…"

The lawyer in her couldn't stop asking more. "What about Mick?"

It was as if a curtain fell as she watched Billy's expression go blank. He stared off into space, not hearing them any longer.

Her mother stroked the old man's arm. "Billy has Alzheimer's. He's been here for the last year. There are days when he talks, then there are days when he just sits here." Claire sighed. "Billy has talked more with you today than he has in a very long time."

The attendant arrived and took charge of Billy, pushing his wheelchair down the hall. Paige stared after them recalling the old man's words.

"Mom, what did Billy mean about an accident?"

"I'm not sure," her mother answered as they walked toward the door. "Billy rambles a lot. It could have been something that happened years ago, or recently."

Paige knew that Billy Hutchinson had an interest in several silver mines in the area. And it was a fact that he hadn't always been fair about his business dealings.

"Not only had the Hutchinson family founded Destiny, but they've been pretty forceful in their efforts to control it," Claire said. "Maybe in Billy's advanced years, he wants to atone for his sins."

Paige wasn't the optimist her mother was; she knew the man was a schemer, because she had gotten talked into one of them. For ten years no one had ever known Paige's connection to Billy. And she wanted to keep it that way. She couldn't see the man again.

But all the way home old Billy's words bothered her. Was there more to his ramblings? The word "accident" kept nagging at her brain. Could Reed's suspicions be truth? Could Billy Hutchinson know more about what really happened the night Mick Larkin disappeared than he previously admitted?

Five hours later, the four exhausted Keenan women, Claire, Morgan, Paige and Leah, collapsed into the chairs at Francisco's Cantina in Durango. Numerous bags pushed under the table were the result of their shopping labors.

Leah smiled brightly. "Did I tell you this is where Holt brought me on our first date?"

"Yes," the other three women said in unison.

Leah pouted and her mother patted her hand. "It's okay, honey, we're just teasing you. We love hearing about it all. You've found a wonderful man and you're going to be married soon. You should be beaming with happiness."

Tears filled Leah's eyes. "Oh, Mom, it's just that I'm so happy. I love Holt so much."

Paige had to turn away. She was glad for her sister, but another side of her envied Leah's happiness. It was something she would never have with her baby's father.

Paige released a long breath as she picked up the menu and scanned it. That didn't mean she couldn't make a good life for her and her child. She didn't need a man to make a living. She was determined to give her baby enough love to make up for his or her father's absence. And it was time she started.

Paige closed the menu and placed it on the table. "I have an announcement, too," she said, drawing the three women's eager attention. "I've decided not to return to my job in Denver. I want to open a law office here…in Destiny."

"Oh, Paige…that's wonderful." Leah jumped up, pulled Paige to her feet and hugged her. "We'll all be living here."

Paige caught Morgan's smile, too. "We're glad to have you back home. So you're going to take the storefront in the town square?"

Morgan and Claire exchanged a look. "You knew about this?" she asked.

Paige held up a hand. "When I talked with Morgan yesterday I hadn't decided yet." She turned to Leah. "I kept quiet because I didn't want anything to overshadow your wedding."

"Oh, Paige. I don't care. I'm just so happy you're moving back."

Paige felt relieved to have shared at least part of her news. "I know. I've missed the family so much." *And I'm going to need all of you when the baby comes, she cried silently.*

"We've all missed you," her mother said as she squeezed Paige's hand. "Your father is going to be so happy."

"What am I going to be happy about?"

They all turned to see Tim Keenan approaching the table. The big man was dressed in a dark blue sport shirt and taupe colored trousers.

Claire slipped her arm around her husband's waist. "Tim, Paige has some wonderful news."

Holt walked up behind Tim and went to his excited bride-to-be then hugged her. "What news?" he echoed.

Paige felt herself blush at the attention. She hated that she hadn't told her family the entire story. Before she could say anything, another man approached the table. Reed Larkin. He was wearing a wine-colored shirt with dark trousers. She'd had no idea he was going to be here, but she was suddenly glad.

Paige gave him a pleading look. He seemed to read her thoughts and went to her side of the table.

"Don't keep us in suspense." Reed smiled.

"It's not that big a deal," she began. "I've decided to try private practice…here in Destiny."

"Oh, lass," her father cried and came around the table to hug her. "I'm so happy. Now, I have all my girls home."

"I love you, Daddy." She hadn't called him that since she was a little girl. Tim Keenan had always made her feel so loved…and so special. The last thing she ever wanted to do was disappoint him.

"It looks like we have a lot to celebrate tonight," he said as he sat down beside his wife.

"Let's just focus on the wedding for now," Paige said. "I took a month's leave from my job so I could think about my decision. I have plenty of time to help Leah with the preparations for her day."

Reed sat down in the only available seat right next to hers. Paige couldn't help but wonder if her sisters had arranged for that to happen. She hoped not.

Reed didn't need to be involved with her and all her baggage. Besides, she'd given up all chances with him many years ago. She stole a glance at him. He was definitely more handsome as a man than he'd been as a boy. Darn her hormones for making her notice, for making her feel something. She didn't need another complication right now.

But more came when the waiter arrived to take their drink orders. Paige ordered a ginger ale with lime, hoping no one questioned her passing on alcohol. No one did, especially when Reed ordered the same, saying he was on duty later that night.

After the waiter left, her father asked, "Have you decided where you want your office?"

"Yesterday I looked at the vacant storefront next to the real estate office. That's where I ran into Reed. He thought I was a vandal."

Everyone turned to Reed. "You can't be too careful."

Holt chuckled. "Yeah, we're overrun with crime in Destiny."

Before Reed could comment, Tim asked, "Doesn't Lyle Hutchinson own that building?"

Paige wasn't surprised. The Hutchinson family owned a lot of property in town square. It was well-known that Billy Hutchinson's son, Lyle, wasn't the best landlord.

"If you want any work done on the building," Morgan said, "you'd better plan to do it yourself."

"The place isn't so bad," Paige said. "It's a perfect space for what I have in mind, and there's even an apartment upstairs." She shrugged. "I don't mind the work. And I have a lot of family to help paint." She glanced at Holt. "And a brand-new brother-in-law."

Holt groaned. "Leah already has me working on the ranch house." He glanced at his friend. "Reed's the expert on remodeling. You should see how he's redone his mother's house."

Reed noticed Paige tense at Holt's suggestion. He didn't take it personally. What with a new career and…a baby on the way, her life was complicated enough. But he couldn't help but feel protective of her, wanting nothing more than to get a hold of the jerk that had deserted her. He'd like to teach him a lesson or two.

"Hey," he said. "If you find you need help, I can paint walls and sand floors."

She looked at him. "Thank you, Reed. First I have to discuss the rental agreement with Lyle. I might not be able to afford the place."

Her mother laughed. "If you handle Lyle like you did Billy this morning, he'll probably agree to your terms without argument."

Reed frowned. "You talked with Billy Hutchinson?"

"Only for a few minutes," Paige said, suddenly feeling guilty. "My mother saw him in the lounge when we left Sally's room. I just stopped by to say hello."

"Billy recognized Paige right away," Claire

said. "And he just began chattering away. It was more than I've heard him say in a long time."

A familiar sinking feeling overcame Reed as he leaned toward Paige. "We need to talk…later."

The waiter arrived to take their order. Paige didn't look pleased, but Reed couldn't let this go. His only link to his father's disappearance was Billy Hutchinson. Reed was almost afraid to hope, but this was the best news he'd had in a long time.

Now, if he could just get Paige to help him.

CHAPTER THREE

BY THE end of the evening, Paige was positive that the members of her family were playing matchmakers. Her mother practically insisted Paige ride back from Durango with Reed, and she didn't protest.

In the passenger seat of Reed's late model truck, she planned ways on how she'd set her family straight. There was no future for her and Reed. What if she just came out and told them she was pregnant with another man's baby?

With a sigh, she leaned back against the headrest and closed her eyes, happy that Reed also seemed to enjoy the quiet, too. Drowsiness took over and she let the soothing vibration of the road lull her. All Paige's problems were temporarily erased from her mind as she recalled the pleasant evening with her family…and Reed.

Paige thought back to the shy, thin boy. How he'd walk her home from school and they would sit at the Keenan kitchen table and do homework while his mother cleaned the guest rooms upstairs. Sometimes they'd go outside and look for toads along the creek. They'd talked sometimes, about how it hurt him when people said things about his father. A lot of people in town had decided Mick Larkin was a thief and had run out on his family.

Besides her sisters, Reed Larkin had been Paige's best friend. But things changed when they went into high school. Girls started noticing tall, good-looking Reed, and other boys had shown interest in Paige.

Reed didn't like it and he'd told her so. Then he kissed her for the first time. She'd been surprised by the strong feelings he invoked in her.

No one could kiss like Reed Larkin.

"Paige…"

She heard Reed's husky voice calling to her. She blinked and finally opened her eyes to be met by Reed's dark gaze as he leaned toward her. She quickly realized her dream had definitely become a reality. And she couldn't resist him.

"Reed…" She reached for him.

Then she felt the soft caress against her lips. A too-brief touch of his mouth on hers, but it was enough to send her heart racing. Unable to stop, Paige turned her head toward him and the kiss deepened…grew bolder. She felt the tip of his tongue against her lips. With a whimper she opened and let him slip inside to taste her.

Wanting more, Paige slid her arms around his neck and combed her fingers into his thick hair. She opened to his caresses and returned his fervor as she stroked her tongue against his. It had never been like this before... she'd never wanted anyone like this. She struggled to get closer.

Abruptly he pulled back, looking pleased with himself. "I have to say your kissing skills have improved since high school."

She shoved at him to see they were parked in the Inn's parking lot. "Get away from me. You took advantage of the situation. I was half asleep," she lied.

"You whispered my name. What's a guy to think?"

Embarrassed, she worked at straightening her clothes. "You're supposed to be a gentleman."

She heard his sigh. "You're right. I apologize."

He stared out the windshield. "Let's just say we were both curious as to what it would be like after all these years."

"Reed, I'm pregnant," she said, barely holding it together. The last thing she wanted to do was fall apart. "I can't afford the luxury to be curious…" Tears clogged her throat, but she swallowed them. "My baby is all I can think about."

"I'm sorry, Paige." He paused. "So the baby's father isn't going to be a part of your life?"

"No. I realized too late, he was never really in my life," she admitted. "It's better this way. Look, I've got to go in." She went for the door handle when he reached for her and stopped her. Somehow she ended up back against him.

Reed had never felt anything as natural as having Paige in his arms. "I'm sorry, Paige. Not because the guy's gone from your life, but because he treated you so badly. You don't deserve that." His hand moved soothingly over her back. "It's going to be all right, honey. Just let me hold you. Nothing more. No pressure…just lean on a friend."

She finally released a trembling sigh and buried her face against his shirt. Her tough act broke his heart. No matter what had happened to end their relationship, it didn't change the fact that he still cared about her.

"You're better off without the guy…and so is the baby. How can I help?"

She pulled back and gave him a little smile. "Some things I have to do on my own, Reed."

"And sometimes you have to rely on a friend."

She looked unconvinced. "That kiss—"

"Won't happen again—not unless you want it, too," he told her. He straightened. "Look, Paige, I'm content with my job. I came back here to make a life, but that doesn't mean it's easy for me to deal with the past." He saw her surprised look. "And yes, I'm still searching for clues about my father's disappearance."

"Reed, it was so long ago."

"I can't give up, Paige." He studied her for a long time. "I need your help. You talked with Billy today."

She nodded. "But...but he didn't say much."

Reed rested his arm on the steering wheel. "Look, Paige, Billy Hutchinson was the last person to see my father the night he disappeared. He also accused Mick of stealing from him. So whatever comes out of his mouth might have meant something."

Paige nodded, then began to repeat everything she remembered Billy had said to her—that he'd thought all lawyers were crooks, and to stay away from all Larkins.

Even with his FBI training, it was hard for Reed to stay objective. "What else?"

Paige frowned. "Billy looked sad and said, 'We can't change the past. Can't change a dang thing...what's done is done.'" Paige studied Reed's face. "His final words were, 'I didn't mean to. It was an accident.'"

"What was an accident?" Reed demanded.

"I asked him the same thing, and Billy just mumbled, 'Mick.' Then he just stared into space."

"Damn, don't you see Paige? Billy had something to do with Dad's disappearance."

During the following week, Paige was busy helping with wedding plans, but she had time to think about Reed, and their kiss.

It was a waste of time. She needed to think about her move…her career…her future. That was why she'd made an appointment with the Realtor about the storefront property.

Paige was doing another walk-through of the space, and she was growing more excited about starting up her own law practice.

"So the floors will be refinished and the walls painted by the end of next week," Paige clarified in her best lawyer tone. "It's imperative that I move in by the first of the month."

"There shouldn't be a problem, Paige." Kaley Sims jotted down notes on her pad. "Lyle is anxious to have this property rented. He'll agree to your requests."

Paige remembered the pretty blonde from high school. Kaley had been in Leah's class. Paige had heard that she was divorced and had a little girl.

"We can have it added into your contract."

Paige raised an eyebrow. "Good. If these upgrades aren't finished in time, Mr. Hutchinson will have to forfeit my security deposit. And I'll have the work done myself, or find another property that is suitable."

Kaley's eyes widened. "Listen to you. A lawyer now and opening an office right here in Destiny. It's going to be so wonderful. Are you going be taking on all kinds of cases?"

Paige nodded. "A general practice, but I

specialized in criminal law since school, but now it's Door Law. Anything that comes through the door."

Kaley looked interested. "Do you go after ex-husbands who don't pay child support?"

Paige tensed, thinking that it was hard for single mothers. "If that's what you need."

"When you hang up your sign, I'll be your first client."

Paige smiled, then glanced around the second-story apartment. "Then get these floors refinished so I can move in."

"Will do."

They went downstairs and walked toward the front door when Reed stepped inside the building. "Hi, Paige." He looked at the blonde and nodded. "Kaley."

"Hey, good-lookin'," Kaley said. "I haven't seen you in a while."

"I've been around, mostly working," Reed said, looking uncomfortable.

Paige watched the quick exchange. Did these two have a past? Was Reed dating her? Paige quickly pushed the thought away. It was none of her business.

"Well, you know what they say," Kaley said. "All work and no play makes you a dull boy…" She gave him a bold once-over. "Haven't seen you at the Silver Bullet in a while."

"Like I said, I've been working."

This time Kaley looked uncomfortable. "Well, I better get back to work." She turned to Paige. "I'll have a crew out here tomorrow." She nodded to Reed and walked out the door.

"So you decided to take the place," Reed said as he glanced around the neglected building.

"There isn't much choice of office space in Destiny." She shrugged. "I took a two-year lease, in exchange for Lyle getting the repairs done and cheaper rent." Paige couldn't resist a chance to tease him. "But after the way you rebuffed Kaley, I'm not sure they'll get done now."

He glared at her. "There's nothing between us. All that happened was one night I ran into her at a bar and bought her a drink."

Paige tried hard to smile. Why did she care so much? "Did I ask?"

He strolled across the room to her. "You wanted to know, though."

"In your dreams, Larkin."

He leaned closer. "Oh, brown-eyes, don't you know, you've been there for years."

Paige sucked in a breath. "How can that be?"

He shrugged. "Do we ever forget the first?"

"Surely you've had other relationships…"

"You want to know if I lived as a monk for the past ten years. Hell, no!" His dark gaze blazed. "But if you want to know if I ever stopped wondering why you pushed me out of your life. Why you suddenly dumped our plans for the future? The answer is, *yes*."

Paige closed her eyes. "I can't give you the answer you want, Reed," she almost begged. "I can't."

He leaned closer. "I'm not buying it, Paige. We meant something to each other. I didn't believe it then and I'm not now." With that he turned and walked out.

Reed called himself every kind of fool as he walked into his office at the sheriff's station. Why had he said anything to Paige? Hell, until that minute he hadn't even realized how much he'd thought about her over the years.

But it was true. He had thought about her. Often. No matter that she'd ripped his heart out. He still couldn't get her out of his head, or his heart. Now, Paige Keenan was back…in his town and his life. And he couldn't seem to stay out of hers.

He picked up his phone messages and carried them back to his office and shut the door. He needed quiet to clear his head of Paige. But he didn't think that was possible.

Hell, she'd been there as long as he could remember.

Even when she was pregnant with another man's baby, he couldn't resist her, resist helping her…kissing her. But he doubted she would take any kind of assistance. She was the most stubborn, independent woman he'd ever met.

Now, other memories fought to surface. His partner in the FBI, Trish Davidson. If he'd ever had feelings for another woman it had been Trish. They'd shared a lot on assignments. There'd been times when they'd been asked to take on the role of husband and wife. Times when the acting as a couple seemed so natural. Familiar pain constricted his chest, making it hard to breathe. It had all fallen apart the day he couldn't save her.

Reed dropped in the chair behind his desk. He had no business trying to play anyone's hero. The past had proved he was lousy at it.

He needed to stop thinking about women and concentrate on what had brought him back to Destiny. His own family and finding out what happened to Mick. He glanced at the picture on the wall. It was the last one of his father and himself taken at the silver mine, Mick's Dream.

After hearing what Billy said to Paige, Reed was sure the man knew what happened to Mick.

Reed clenched his jaw. "Beware, Billy Hutchinson, I haven't given up, and I'm coming after you."

"Everything looks perfect, Paige," Dr. York said as she walked into her office, carrying a file with the test results. "The fetus is healthy and as far as I can tell, so are you."

Paige let out a sigh, not realizing she'd been holding her breath. "That's good."

"Just continue to eat right and no caffeine or alcohol. I also suggest that you exercise to alleviate the stress, especially if you're planning to work during your pregnancy?"

"Yes. I'm opening a private practice in Destiny to be closer to my family."

"So the baby's father isn't going to be involved?"

Paige looked down at her hands. How many more times did she have to answer that question? "No. We're not together. It was his decision."

Dr. York sighed. "Then it's probably better for both you and the child." She looked over the file again. "It states here that Reed Larkin referred you." She smiled. "He's a nice guy. He helped his sister during her pregnancy when her husband was deployed overseas."

Paige nodded. "He's a friend of the family."

"Can't have too many friends. And they make great baby-sitters, too."

Paige thought about her family. She would need all their help to raise this child. "I have sisters."

"Good. Sounds like you have a great support group." The doctor stood. "If you have any questions just call the office, and I'll see you next month."

After they shook hands, Paige walked out and through the busy waiting room. She couldn't help but place her hand over her stomach protectively. There wasn't any movement yet, but there would be soon. She smiled. For the first time she allowed herself to rejoice over the fact that she had a life growing inside of her. A baby.

Suddenly she longed to share the news with someone. With that decision in mind, she headed to her car and back to Destiny. To her family.

* * *

"You're pregnant…" Morgan breathed.

Paige nodded from across her sister's desk. She had given her sister a brief synopsis of her situation, before the news. "It's not something I planned. I thought we had a serious relationship." Her voice grew soft. "He didn't feel the same."

"Oh, Paige…"

"I would have told you, and Mom and Dad right away, but I didn't want to take anything away from Leah's wedding. But after my doctor's visit, I'm about to burst with the news."

"So you just handled this all on your own. You went to the doctor alone…" Morgan came around the desk and pulled Paige into her arms. "I hate that you've had to go through this by yourself."

"Well…not entirely. Reed discovered the news right away. He helped me." Tears flooded Paige's eyes. "He gave me the name of his sister's doctor." She smiled but it didn't stop the waterworks and Morgan was there to hold her. "I'm okay, really, it's just these darn hormones…I cry at everything."

"You can cry all you want," Morgan said. "I'm here. What do you need me to do, outside of putting a hit on one Denver detective?"

Paige pulled away. "He's not worth it," she said. "It's just that I feel like such a fool for falling for his lies."

"You loved him."

Maybe once, Paige thought, but whatever she'd felt for Drew had died with his lies and deceit. "I'll get over it. This baby is my only concern right now. That's why I'm moving back home. It's important my child has family around."

"This is so wonderful. A baby." Her older sister's green eyes lit up. "I'm going to be an aunt." She gasped. "Mom and Dad are going to be grandparents."

Paige sank down in her chair. "How are they going to handle this news?"

"Like they have everything else, with open arms," Morgan assured her. "What they won't like is that you didn't go to them right away."

Paige knew she was right. "I'll tell them as soon as the wedding is over. I want Leah to have her special day."

"You're lucky that it's only two days away. All you have to get through is the rehearsal dinner and the day of the wedding."

Paige wasn't worried about the ceremony, but that she'd be spending that time with Reed.

Paige stood up at the head table and tapped her knife against her water glass to get the attention of about fifty guests in the Keenan Inn's dining room.

The murmurs died out as Paige glanced at Reed looking entirely too handsome in his black tux. He smiled his encouragement and she swallowed before she looked at Leah and her new husband, Holt Rawlins.

"I have to tell you I'm standing here because I won the coin flip." She smiled as chuckles filled the room. "As all of you know the Keenan sisters are close. And although we've been apart the past few years that closeness never wavered. Now, Leah has added a man into the mix." Her smile widened. "But all I have to do is see the way these two look at each other to know they're in love. And Leah isn't just getting a new husband…but a son, too. Holt and Corey, I think you both know how lucky you are to have Leah."

Paige raised her glass of sparkling cider. "To Holt and Leah…may their happiness and love grow through the years."

As she drank from her glass, she felt Reed

come up behind her, pressing his hand against her back.

"Now, it's my turn," he said as he looked at the bride and groom.

"As you all know Holt has only lived here a short time. A New Yorker who was going to run a ranch and make a life here." The crowd laughed. "We thought he'd never work out. He proved us wrong. He had guts, and learned to ride and brand cattle with ease, but he had his hands full with Leah Keenan. The sparks began to fly from the get-go." He raised his glass and looked at the couple. "If I've ever seen two people who belong together, it's you two. Here's to love…and sparks." He took a sip from his glass.

There were more tapping sounds and calls for the bride and groom to kiss. They did.

Paige continued to smile when a sudden dizziness hit her. She swayed but felt Reed's hand grip her waist.

"I got you." His grip tightened at her waist as he led her through the door and into the hall. They smiled at guests, then continued walking until they got outside and the cooler air hit her. Paige sucked in a long breath as they walked the length of the wraparound porch toward the back of the Inn. He sat her down at one of the tables and pressed her head down to her knees.

"Take a deep breath," he told her, then left her momentarily. When he returned she felt a cool cloth against her neck. After a few minutes Paige raiscd her head, feeling somewhat better.

He looked concerned. "How do you feel?"

"Better, thanks."

He took off his jacket and wrapped it around her shoulders to ward off the cool evening temperature. He squatted down in front of her. If possible his shoulders looked wider in his pleated white shirt, even with the bow tie.

"I feel so silly."

"It's been a long day," he said. "You probably haven't been off your feet in hours."

"I have to go back inside."

His ebony gaze narrowed at her. "Says who?"

"I'm the maid of honor. I'm supposing to be attending to the bride."

"I think Holt is giving his bride enough attention." He tugged the jacket tighter around her. "It's you who needs a little TLC and I intend to do that."

Paige started to deny it when the sound of voices caused her to glance over his shoulder. "People are looking at us."

"So, they'll just think we're out here to be alone."

"Everyone will believe there's something between us."

He frowned. "Well, don't act like that's such a bad thing."

"I didn't mean it like that." She placed her

hand on his arm. "It's just my…condition. People might think that you're…the father."

His gaze held hers; she couldn't pull away. "Like I said, would that be such a bad thing?"

Paige barely held back her gasp. She didn't want to analyze what Reed was telling her. It would be so easy to lean on him…get used to having him around.

Tears welled in her eyes. "Oh, Reed. You shouldn't say a thing like that.…"

"Why not? I want to tell you a lot of things, Paige. Like how beautiful you look today." He brushed a curl away from her face. "How beautiful you look every day."

"Wait until I get fat.…"

"You're with child, Paige." His hands cupped her face. "You look more incredible… with each passing day." His dark gaze held hers so tenderly. "A lot of men, me included, think that's sexy—"

"Oh, Reed…" She touched his face.

"You're nurturing a new life inside you. That's a pretty special thing…"

Before Paige could speak, she heard her mother's voice.

Paige glanced up to see her parents. "Are you all right?" her mother asked.

She stood. Reed wrapped his arm around her shoulders for support. "We were just getting some air."

Behind her parents, Morgan appeared along with Leah and Holt. "Paige, are you all right?" Leah asked.

Paige glanced at Morgan and her older sister whispered the words. "Tell them."

"Tell us what, honey?" her mother asked.

Tears pooled in Paige's eyes, and she felt Reed's hold tighten. "I wanted to wait until after the wedding…so not to spoil Leah's day, but I guess it's time."

She glanced back and forth between her mother and father. "I'm pregnant."

CHAPTER FOUR

REED stepped back as the Keenan family gathered Paige in a loving embrace. Tears flowed as they hugged and stroked their daughter and sister.

Holt came up beside him, and together they watched the fussing. "I take it you knew about this."

Reed couldn't deny it. "I only discovered it by accident. The day Paige arrived home she fainted, and I was there to catch her." He looked at his friend. "And the last thing Paige wanted to do was overshadow her sister's wedding."

Holt shook his head in disbelief. "Being an only child and from a dysfunctional family that didn't believe in showing any affection, I'm still having a little trouble adjusting to all this togetherness."

"Seems to me you're doing just fine… you already have the beginnings of a nice family."

Holt grinned and puffed out his chest. "Corey is a great kid and a pretty self-sufficient nine-year-old. A baby is a lot different," Holt said. "And a little scary."

Reed wasn't sure he felt that way. He looked at Paige, and an incredible longing came over him. Since high school he'd thought a hundred times about the two of them ending up together. But that seemed like ages ago. Things were different now.

"You'll make a great dad," he told Holt.

"I hope you're right, because Leah wants a baby right away. And after Paige's news, I doubt I can talk her into waiting a while."

A smiling Leah came to her new husband's side. "We should go back in to see to our guests."

Holt kissed her. "You sure? If you want to stay out here with your sister…"

"Oh, no, please," Paige said as she turned around. "I'm fine, really. This is your wedding day. Go!" She waved at the bride and groom.

"Why don't you all go inside," Reed told them. "I'll stay here with Paige." All eyes turned to him.

"Great idea," Paige agreed. "He'll make sure I'm fine."

Her mother hesitated, then said, "Reed would you make sure Paige goes upstairs so she can rest?"

"Sure, Mrs. K."

Paige watched her family walk off, then turned to Reed. "You don't have to baby-sit me. I can make it on my own."

"No go. I promised your mother, so don't make me carry you."

Although annoyed over Reed's bossiness, Paige decided not to test his words. To avoid any of the lingering guests, she followed the porch around and went in through the kitchen. The caterers were busy cleaning as she walked to the back staircase and Reed followed her. She had no doubt by tomorrow everyone would have them linked romantically.

On the third floor she headed down the long hall to the large room she'd shared with her sisters. She opened the door and walked into the pale pink room.

Three single beds lined the angled walls, each covered with a handmade quilt. On the other side, a small desk and three dressers were arranged under the dormer windows. There was a shelf filled with high school and college mementos.

She stood next to her bed. "Okay, I've made it. You can leave."

Reed ignored her as he looked around. "So

this is the Keenan sisters' bedroom. Did you know how many guys wanted to end up here?" He grinned. "And look at me, I've made it into the inner sanctum. Wait until I tell Tommy Peterson."

"Knock it off, Larkin." Paige dropped to the bed and kicked off her high-heel shoes. Her wine colored bridesmaid dress dragged on the floor as she walked to the closet, pulled out a pair of sweats and marched into the connecting bath.

"If you need any help just yell," he called out as she slammed the door.

Paige tossed her clothes on the counter and reached behind her, only to realize she couldn't get hold of the zipper. "Damn."

She yanked open the door to find him standing right there. She turned her back at him. "You make any smart remarks and you'll be sorry."

She felt the zipper lower. "I meant what I said earlier, you looked beautiful today."

Paige felt bloated and her dress was too tight. "Thank you." Turning around, she found Reed staring at her.

"You always were, and even more so now." His gaze lowered to her overflowing cleavage.

"Don't say that…I can't deal…"

"It's the truth, Paige. You are beautiful." His hand touched her cheek.

"Oh, Reed." She was losing the battle to stay strong. Why did he always have to be around during her worst moments?

"I'm here, Paige." He pulled her close. "I'm here for you."

She laid her head against his shirt and began to cry. He wrapped her in his arms and held her. It felt so good…too good, and she didn't want to pull away. For a while she wanted to lean on someone. But Reed Larkin wasn't just anyone. He was someone she'd cared about for a lot of years.

And her body seemed to recognize those

feelings. The difference was subtle, but his touch grew intense as he slowly stroked her back, causing her own awareness. She pulled back, but his dark gaze held her, refusing to let her break the connection.

His head lowered to hers, and she was eager to take what he was offering her when the bedroom door swung open and Morgan walked in.

Paige quickly pulled out of Reed's embrace just in time to keep from making another mistake.

A week later, Reed sat in his office, reading his mail. One letter in particular interested him. It was from Lyle Hutchinson's lawyer. Since Billy Hutchinson went into Shady Haven, his only son had taken over all the business affairs. Lyle wanted to buy the Larkin family's share in the Mick's Dream mine. Why now? The mine had been closed since Mick Larkin's disappearance.

Years ago, his father's partner, Billy, had said the mine had been nearly stripped and would cost too much to keep the operation going. Mick had disagreed, and the night he'd disappeared he had confided in his son he'd found the big strike. Mick went out to celebrate that night and never returned home.

The next morning the sheriff had appeared at their door looking for Mick, saying he stole from Billy Hutchinson. Mick hadn't been able to defend himself because they'd never found him. Even during Reed's years in the FBI he'd never turned up anything. And it wasn't for lack of trying. It was as if the man had been abducted by aliens. Reed felt sure his father was dead. And someone had wanted to make sure Mick Larkin was never found.

A knock on his door brought Reed back to reality. His young deputy, Sam Collins, peered inside. He was just six months out of training, but he was enthusiastic. His other deputy, Gary Malvern, had a few more years experience.

"Hey, Reed," Sam greeted him. "You want me out on patrol, or working the desk?"

Checking his watch, Reed folded the paper and stuffed it in his pocket. He stood. "You handle the desk until Gary comes in at noon, then run patrol. I'm heading home. Call me if anything important comes up."

Reed was off-duty, and for the first time in a long time, he had places to go and people to see. First on his list was Paige Keenan, attorney at law.

Paige stood back and looked around at the boxes sitting on the newly stained floors in her office. She never realized how many law books she had accumulated over the years until she'd gotten them out of storage. And she needed every one of them and more if she was going to open her office.

Already two desks and several file cabinets had been delivered that morning. She wanted more furniture in the reception area, along with a rug, some plants and accessories. And when she could afford it, a receptionist.

Paige raised her gaze to the ceiling. Nothing had been done to the apartment upstairs. First, she needed to get her law practice going and make some money. She'd resigned from her job with the D.A. and she didn't want to deplete her entire savings account.

Her hand covered her slightly rounded stomach and she smiled. Now that she'd explained the situation to her parents, they'd been nothing but understanding and loving. Their support was important to her.

Paige's thoughts turned to her childhood, and her biological mother. The mother who brought her and her sisters to Destiny and left them for the Keenans to raise. Had her life been so horrific that she couldn't keep her own children? Claire and Tim Keenan had told the girls that they'd tell them the story when they were old enough to understand. But they never had, and she and her sisters had never insisted. Maybe it was because Morgan, Paige and Leah were afraid to know the truth. Either way, the girls thought of Claire and Tim Keenan as their parents.

Paige couldn't think about that now. She had a practice to set up and went back to pulling books from boxes. As she carried them into the office, she wondered where the kids Morgan had promised to send to help her were.

Paige heard the front door open. Good, help had arrived. "All right, kids," she called. "You can start by bringing boxes back here."

She continued to fill the shelves, but glanced over her shoulder when she heard her help arrive. It wasn't a high school student. It was Reed.

He set a box down on the floor. "Are you paying minimum wage?"

"Of course." Paige smiled and eyed him closely. He looked too good in his worn jeans and blue polo shirt. She hadn't seen him since the night of the wedding and suddenly she realized she had missed him. "Are you applying for a job?"

"I'm off work, so I can give you a few hours."

"I can't ask you…"

"You're not asking, I'm offering. Besides, these boxes are too heavy for you…especially in your condition."

"Morgan's sending some kids by. Some of the football team."

He nodded. "Good. How are you feeling these days?"

"I'm fine. My mother is taking very good care of me. And the doctor said I'm healthy."

He walked to her desk. "So you like Dr. York?"

"She's nice. She also remembers you. Says you were good with Jodi."

He shrugged and sat down on the edge of the large desk. "I was just filling in for her husband." He shook his head. "It was quite an experience."

"Easy for you to say, you were just a by-stander."

Reed couldn't help but stare at Paige. It had been a long week, and he'd missed not seeing her. That wasn't supposed to happen, especially now since her parents were available. But that hadn't stopped him from walking through town square, slowing at her office several times during the week, wondering how she was doing. Even his mother kept mentioning Paige during their visits.

Paige looked away. "I'd better get back to work."

"I'll help, but first, I need yours. I want to be your first client." He pulled out the letter and handed it to her.

After a few minutes, she looked at him. "Do you have any reason to want to keep the mine?"

"Not really."

"How does your mother feel about it?" She raised an eyebrow. "I take it you're handling her business affairs."

He nodded. "I don't want to talk to her about this just yet. I'm more concerned why Lyle suddenly wants the mine. It's been over fifteen years since Mick's Dream was closed. According to Billy, it's not worth anything. And you know as well as I do, the Hutchinsons don't waste their time and money on anything unless it's profitable."

Paige didn't want to get involved with this. But after speaking with Billy that day, she hadn't been able to forget the things he'd said.

"Was there a partnership between your father and Billy? In writing?"

Reed shook his head. "Hutchinson says there's an agreement, but Dad always told us that he'd never give away any part of Mick's Dream. I think my father was tricked into giving up shares. Then the night he disappeared, he told me that he'd found a silver vein. Then he got a phone call from Billy and said he was going to meet with him. That was the last time I saw my father. The next morning the sheriff showed up, saying Billy had accuscd Mick of stealing from him."

Over the years, Paige had heard several versions of the stories. She and Reed had talked about what happened, but they never really knew the details.

"Back then did you tell the sheriff what your father told you about finding the silver vein?"

"Let's just say he wasn't interested in listening to Mick's kid. Not long after that day,

Billy showed up and told Mom that he was closing the mine. He gave her a copy of the agreement Billy and Dad had. It's bogus. I had it tested when I worked for the Bureau. It's not my father's signature."

"Why haven't you gone to the authorities?"

He shrugged. "A lot of reasons. I couldn't drag my mother through this again. Anyway, Billy never pressed charges against my father."

"But you want to reopen it all now. Because Billy said some things to me."

Reed nodded. "And I need you to talk to him again. I know that man is behind Mick's disappearance." His gaze grew intense. "My father wouldn't run out on his family."

"Reed, no jury in the world is going to believe the ramblings of a man with Alzheimer's."

"It's not about pressing charges, Paige. I just want to know the truth. And after all these years, that isn't too much to ask." Those dark eyes bored into hers. "Now my question is, are you willing to take on this case?"

She studied his face for a moment, then said, "I can't, Reed, not if I'm going to help you."

Paige told herself for the hundredth time she had to be crazy. But she had agreed to talk to Billy Hutchinson, because she wanted to help Reed.

What she needed was to avoid the temptation of the man, but she rode out to visit Sally Larkin with her son anyway.

They arrived at the convalescence home and Reed signed in, then they walked down the hall to Sally's room. Reed knocked and opened the door, then went to his mother sitting in the wheelchair.

"Hi, Mom."

Paige watched as mother and son exchanged a hug and a kiss. Then Sally looked in her direction and held out a hand.

Paige went to her. "Hello, Sally. How are you today?"

"Fine." She smiled and glanced at her son. Paige knew that the woman was thinking they were a couple again. And why shouldn't she. They'd been thrown together a lot the past two weeks.

"Good. I brought wedding pictures." Paige sat down beside Sally, and for the next ten minutes went through the reception that Sally hadn't been able to attend.

After a little while, Paige made an excuse to leave and waved her goodbye. She was nervous as she headed toward the lounge. She'd agreed to do this, but insisted Reed tell his mother about Lyle's offer to buy the mine.

Paige walked past Karen at her desk. With an innocent smile Paige waved at the busy director, and strolled into the sitting area. The room was nearly empty, then she spotted the old man in his wheelchair by the open French doors.

Billy.

He was by himself while his attendant stood across the room talking with another employee. As if he recognized her, Billy motioned for her to come over.

Looking around the deserted room, Paige curled her shaky hands into fists and made her way to him.

"You looking for me, young lady?"

She was taken aback by his bluntness. "Sure. How are you, Billy?"

"I'm old and dyin'. Can't get much worst than that."

She forced a smile. "You've lived a long time. And you've accomplished a lot. Built a town, had a family, struck it rich in silver." She'd hoped that was all he remembered, and not their conversation years ago.

The old man's eyes lit up. "Yeah. Those were the good days. I had everything back then. Money… women…friends."

Paige had heard about Billy's prowess. He was shrewd in business and his reputation with women was legendary.

"Now, my son took it all away, and had me locked up in here."

Paige had no doubt that Billy needed to have assisted care. "You have to admit it's very nice here, Billy. And people can come to visit you."

He waved his crippled hand in the air. "Bah, my own boy only comes here so people won't talk. He has all my money and didn't even have to work for it. He's a lazy son of a gun," he growled.

Paige glanced around again, but no one was paying attention to them. She sat down in the chair next to him. "And you worked hard in the mines, didn't you, Billy?"

His eyes narrowed in concentration as if trying to recall. "Day and night. It's back-breaking work, but I finally struck it rich." He grinned. "A few times."

"You worked a lot of years. Weren't you a partner in Mick's Dream?"

The old man stared out into space, and Paige thought he wasn't going to speak. "I had to close it. There was a cave-in…and I lost… Oh, Mick…" He tensed and a panicked look distorted his lined face. "It wasn't my fault. He fought me… He wanted it all." His eyes were pleading as he gripped Paige's hand. "You believe me, don't you? It wasn't my fault."

"Who fought you, Billy?" she asked, trying not to be too insistent. But he didn't answer. His expression suddenly went blank. She'd lost him. Billy Hutchinson had escaped into his own world.

"Excuse me, ma'am."

Paige turned to see the large male attendant. "I need to take Billy back to his room for his nap."

She stood. "I'm sorry."

The young man smiled. "No, please, don't

be. Billy doesn't get many visitors. It's nice that you stopped to talk to him."

She nodded.

The orderly turned the wheelchair toward the exit. "Maybe we'll see you again," he said.

Oh God. Paige's stomach turned over as she stood and headed for the exit. She needed some air. She walked through the door and sucked in a long breath. Had Billy meant he'd accidentally killed Mick Larkin, or were they just the babblings of a sick man? What should she tell Reed?

"Are you all right?"

She jerked around to see Reed. His dark gaze showed his concern. "Get me out of here."

With a nod, Reed helped her into the truck, started the engine and pulled out onto the highway. He wasn't going to ask her now, but the look on Paige's face told him that she'd learned something from Billy. For years, he'd run into dead ends. Reed was sure that Billy Hutchinson was the only one who knew the truth.

He glanced at the exhausted woman beside him. He'd waited a long time for any news…a little while longer wasn't going to kill him.

Later that day, Paige couldn't believe she'd slept so long. She had no idea that being pregnant could make her so tired. Getting off her bed, she went into the bathroom and brushed her teeth, rehashing her visit with Billy this morning.

She had tried many cases in court, and knew what questions to ask, but she couldn't seem to interrogate an old man with Alzheimer's. But, in her gut, she knew that Billy had something to do with Mick Larkin's disappearance. And she had to tell Reed.

She ran a brush through her hair and applied some lipstick. She didn't want to keep the information to herself any longer. When he'd dropped her at the Inn, he told her he was off-duty and would be at home. So that was where she had to go.

The Larkin home had never been a showcase. A small run-down bungalow on an acre of land. Mick Larkin had spent all his extra time and money working in Mick's Dream. She pulled off the main street to be pleasantly surprised. The brick and wood structure had been refurbished with a new roof and paint. The lawn was manicured and rows of colorful plants lined the walkway.

Paige climbed the three new wooden steps to the porch. The solid oak door had been stained a dark color. It looked like Reed had been busy since returning to Destiny. She rang the bell and waited.

Finally the door opened, but to Paige's surprise it wasn't Reed, but a woman. A very pretty woman. Jealousy reared inside her as the dark-haired beauty smiled at her.

"I'm…I'm looking for Reed Larkin."

"And you found the right place." The woman's smile widened more. "This is Reed's house, but he's in the shower."

Paige backed away. So there was someone in his life. "I'll just come back at a more convenient time."

"No, you won't, Paige Keenan." The young woman reached for her. "You don't remember me, do you? I'm Jodi. Reed's kid sister."

Paige blinked. "Jodi? Little Jodi."

"I kind of grew up."

"You're beautiful."

"As compared to the little ragamuffin I used to be."

Jodi was a lot younger than Reed and Paige. Sally had put her in day care while working. "Oh, no. It's just when we went to college, you were so young. I didn't recognize you."

"You haven't changed at all," she told Paige. "Please come inside. Reed will be out of the shower soon."

Paige stepped inside the living room with the gleaming hardwood floors and snowy-white moldings. The walls were painted a taupe and the furniture looked new, except for some of the wooden pieces.

"The room looks great. Reed must have worked hard to redo the place."

"Yes, he did." Jodi motioned for her to follow her. "Come into the kitchen. That's my favorite room." A wall had been knocked out connecting the dining room to the kitchen where all new cherry wood cabinets lined the walls, and granite countertops glistened along with the stainless steel appliances.

"Pretty impressive, huh?"

"Reed did this?"

She nodded. "He wants it nice for Mom to come home to." The sound of a baby crying erupted in the silence. "And that's my man calling to me. Reed should be here in a minute. Coming, Nicky," Jodi called as she walked out.

Paige should go. She could call Reed and tell him what Billy had said. She walked around the counter, her hand traced the granite as she looked closely at the travertine backsplash. This place made her condo look downright tacky.

"Jodi, where are my clean clothes?" Reed's voice echoed into the room right before he appeared in the doorway. He looked just as startled to see her as she was to see him. "Paige?"

Paige swallowed hard as she stared at the wide shoulders and well-developed chest. Her pulse started to speed up as her gaze lowered to the towel that was the only thing that covered his magnificent body.

CHAPTER FIVE

AFTER Reed slipped on his jeans, he pulled a T-shirt over his head. He didn't mess with shoes as he headed back to the kitchen before Paige ran off. To say he'd been surprised that she'd come to the house was an understatement.

Reed walked into the kitchen and found Paige seated at the granite counter along with his sister and little Nicholas. It was like a punch in his gut to see Paige holding the baby. She looked so…natural.

Jodi was the first to notice his return. "I see you've managed to find some clothes," she said, with a sly smile.

"No thanks to you. If you'd leave my clothes alone, I'd know where to find them."

"You mean on the floor."

"I was sorting them for the wash."

Jodi grinned. "And that's your story and you're sticking to it."

"You got that right." Reed went to the refrigerator and pulled out a soda. "Paige, can I offer you something to drink?"

"No, thank you." She cooed at the baby. "I got my hands full."

Reed came to see little Nick. At six months old, the boy had grown like a weed. He gave his uncle a toothy grin and raised his arms up to be held. Reed put down his drink, and lifted him into his arms. He loved this little guy and had had the opportunity to be a stand-in dad. But when he'd come home today, he wasn't in the mood for company—not his sister's anyway.

"As you can see, Jodi invades my peace on

the weekends. She tries to organize my things and my life."

"Only because you need organizing," Jodi told him.

"Can't wait until big Nick comes home so you'll leave me alone."

"Eight more weeks," Jodi breathed as she smiled at her brother. "And you're going to miss us."

He glanced at Paige and winked. "Maybe not so much. Besides, you're only as far away as Durango."

Jodi turned to Paige this time. "I try to visit Mom as much as possible. She loves seeing Nicolas."

"I bet she does," Paige said as she let Nicky grasp her finger. "I've gotten to visit Sally a few times. She seems to be doing well, and the home is such a nice place."

"Thanks to Reed. He makes sure Mom has the best of care."

"Jodi…" He didn't want to broadcast it.

"Well, you do." His sister stood and kissed him on the cheek. "You're the best brother a girl could have."

"I'm the only brother you got." Reed handed her the baby. "I think he needs a diaper change."

Jodi wrinkled her nose. "I should say so. Come on, big guy, your mama needs to change you." She glanced over her shoulder. "Paige, why don't you stay for dinner. Reed's barbecuing." Without waiting for an answer, she left them alone.

Paige looked at him. "Oh, I can't interrupt your family time…"

Reed shrugged. "Like I haven't been eating at your family's table a few times." Call him crazy, but he wanted her here…with him. "Besides, we have some things to discuss."

She nodded. "I'll call Mom so she won't worry." She reached into her purse for her cell phone.

Reed's hand covered hers. "Paige, I want you to know how much I appreciate what you're doing."

She nodded. "I just don't know if it'll help."

"You're helping by just coming here." That could be a lie. Paige was distracting him, but she always had.

"What are friends for?"

Jodi had been a little too obvious, going to bed just after eight o'clock. Maybe it was a good thing because Reed wasn't ready to let his sister in on what was going on. She had been just a kid when their dad had gone missing. He didn't want to drag her through anything yet, not until he had more facts.

Reed carried two glasses of lemonade out to the back deck. The sun had gone down and the evening was cooling off. The sound of crickets filled the air along with the clean scent of the pines.

"Are you warm enough?" He handed Paige her glass.

"I'm fine," she said. "It's so peaceful here. I really missed this living in Denver."

Reed sat down in the teakwood chair next to Paige, realizing too late it was a mistake to sit so close. He was far too aware of the woman. Hell, he could be in the next room and he'd still be aware of her.

He stretched his legs out in front of him. "I finished the deck about a month ago. Mom bugged Dad for years to build one, but he never quite got around to it."

Paige took a sip. "It's easy to put things off."

He sighed. It was time to get down to business. "I've never stopped trying to find my dad, Paige. You, better than anyone, know the promise I made myself. All the years I had to see my mother's pain…"

"I know, Reed. And I want to help."

He turned toward her. "Then tell me what Billy said to you."

She continued to stare into the night. "He said no one comes to visit him, not even his son."

"So Lyle isn't the dutiful son." Reed took a sip of his drink. "Just when it comes to handling the money. Then doesn't it seem strange that Billy's son wants to buy out a worthless mine?" he murmured more to himself than to her.

"I asked Billy if he had any mines now. He said he had one, but he had to close it. Said there was a cave-in."

Reed didn't remembered a cave-in. Had something happened after his father's disappearance? "Billy never went back into the mine. No one did. He closed Mick's Dream immediately after he accused Dad of robbing him." The man was lying, or he was confused. "Sorry. What else did he say?"

"Like I said, he told me there was a cave-in." Paige looked at him. "Then Billy said, *I lost... Oh, Mick...* Billy shook his head and looked like he was in pain. *It wasn't my fault*, he cried. *He fought me... He wanted it all.*" Paige's gaze held his. "Those were his exact words."

"What wasn't his fault?" Reed asked.

Paige shook her head. "I'm not sure. Billy repeated it again, and kept asking if I believed him."

Reed took a drink from his glass. Had Billy killed his father? Where was the body? The mine had been searched.

"Reed, I'm a lawyer and I have to deal in facts. But I think Billy was trying to tell me something." She raised her hand. "I say this because Billy also told me that his son had him locked away." She paused.

"Don't stop now," Reed coaxed.

"Okay this is just speculation. But what if

Billy told these things to Lyle? What if in his confused mind he confessed something to his son? Something about your father."

"You mean like what really happened that night?"

"What do you think happened that night, Reed?"

For years, he wanted to believe his father was alive, but as an adult, after years with the FBI, he dealt in facts, too. "I think Billy and Mick fought that night. And Dad…died."

Reed cursed and jumped up from his chair. He hated this. He wanted it all to end—to be finished for good.

Paige came up beside him. "Reed, you know as well as I do that you can't open an investigation based on the words of an Alzheimer's patient."

"Suddenly you're acting as my lawyer."

"No, as your friend."

"So Billy just gets away with it? Lyle gets

to bury the secret when his dad dies. The Hutchinsons get to keep their good name, and the hell with the Larkins."

"No. But you still only have Billy's words. Reed, you've made a good name in this town. People respect you."

"I don't care about me. It's my mother and my father. She needs this to end. If I can't give her anything else, I want to give her some peace at this time in her life. Do you realize what she had to endure the last seventeen years? How hard she had to work? And I went off to college and left her."

Paige grabbed his arm and made him look at her. "Your mother wanted you to go to college more than anything. It was all she could give you. You would be surprised what a mother can give her child out of love." She blinked at the tears in her eyes. "And Sally Larkin loves her children. Your only way to better your circumstance was through college and she knew that. So don't ever think that you should have given that up. She wanted a better life for you and for Jodi."

"So did Dad. The night he disappeared, he told me he'd found the big silver vein." Reed's voice was tight with emotion. "He wanted to give his family things, too. A better life for his wife and kids. Dammit! And Billy Hutchinson, with his greed, put an end to a man's dreams."

"No matter how much we want to, Reed." She sighed. "We can't go back."

"It's funny, we've come right back…right back here to Destiny. Do you ever think about what would have happened between us if we hadn't broken up?"

Paige glanced away. "That was a long time ago, Reed. We were kids and college was the best thing for both of us."

"I know, we planned to go together," he reminded her. "Or I was going to follow you to Denver." He was going to work a year or so, then attend college. When a special scholarship came through for school back east, he hadn't wanted to take it—until Paige told him that it would be better if they went their separate ways.

"It worked out for the best."

He leaned toward her. The same feelings he'd felt for her then still stirred inside him now. Not a damn thing had changed for him when it came to Paige Keenan. Even after all this time, the questions still haunted him. And he needed an answer.

"Paige, you never did tell me what I did to make you stop loving me."

She immediately looked surprised at his direct question. "Reed, it was so long ago."

"Not that long ago. Not when we were so in love…we could barely keep our hands off each other." He had never taken things too far with Paige.

He still respected her now, but his hunger overtook his common sense. He reached for her. "It still is, Paige. When I look at you now all those years disappear." He bent his head and brushed a kiss across her mouth. She gasped and her eyes widened in desire. She could never hide that from him. He leaned down and captured her mouth in a hungry kiss.

She gave a tiny whimper and wrapped her arms around his neck and kissed him back. He brought her up against him, and reveled in her feel, her taste…

He decided then and there, he'd never gotten her out of his system…and most likely never would.

Over the next couple of weeks, Paige buried herself in organizing her new law office. She planned to officially open her doors in two weeks. Although the disarray hadn't seemed to matter to the six new clients who'd just walked in from the street in the last few days. As promised, Kaley Sims was there in line for her services.

Paige had also taken a job one day a week in family court in Durango. At least she'd be able to until the baby was born. She frowned. That had her thinking about the still bare apartment upstairs. She thought about her furniture still in Denver as she walked out of her office, and climbed the stairs.

The living quarters had greatly improved. All the walls were painted an eggshell. The kitchen cabinets had been repaired, and Paige had replaced the old knobs with brushed nickel, matching the new faucet and light fixture over the sink. It looked ready to move in.

That meant she had to go to Denver, and arrange for a moving van to put her things in storage. She'd decided to just rent her condo for now. In fact, one of her co-workers had needed a place to live.

Paige rubbed her temples. She wasn't looking forward to returning to Denver. Morgan had offered to go with her and help her pack up. How could she pack up nearly eight years of her life there, nearly five with the D.A.?

And what if she ran into Drew?

Paige knew she had to have contact with him one more time, then he would be out of her life and the baby's life for good. And she could move on. She didn't need a man in her life. She wasn't exactly high on trusting another man anytime soon.

Paige's thoughts turned to what Reed had said the other night. What if things had turned out differently? What if she hadn't broken up with him? Maybe they could have made it together. Back then she'd loved Reed enough. But he needed a chance at a future. And the only way she could guarantee that had been to break up with him, so he'd accept his scholarship.

Although they'd been determined to make it together, they were too young and the odds were against them. Paige shook away the thought. Nothing could change the past.

She wasn't going to think about regrets now. As awful as Drew had been about her pregnancy, Paige already loved this baby. They had each other…and that had to be enough for now.

Reed called out to Paige as he came through the office front door. When he didn't find her downstairs, he decided to try the apartment. He climbed the steps and saw her standing at the row of windows. She was dressed in a pair of black stretch pants and an oversize print blouse. Her hair was pulled back into a ponytail. She looked about eighteen.

"Paige," he breathed.

With a gasp, she swung around. "Reed! Why do you always have to startle me?"

"I wasn't trying to," he told her as he climbed the last few steps. "I called to you, but I guess you didn't hear me. Sorry."

She sighed. "I guess I was daydreaming."

He glanced around the empty room. "Was furniture involved?"

"I have furniture, I just need to get it here."

"You need some help?"

She stared at him. "You need a life, Larkin, if you want to spend your free time moving furniture."

Reed hadn't thought about his personal life in a long time. He'd been pretty busy between work and taking care of his mother, and the family home. But since Paige's return, he realized how empty his life was. How he'd come to the conclusion, especially after a series of earth-shattering kisses, he'd never stopped caring about her. "What I don't want is for you to move furniture."

"I'm not. I plan to store most of it, and buy some new. I still have to go to Denver."

"Sounds like you have everything under control."

Paige didn't have anything under control, especially when this man was around. So how could she think she'd loved one man a few months ago, then suddenly get feelings for another? This one she couldn't blame on hormones.

"It's how it's got to be for me." Somehow she had to keep Reed out of her life...her heart. "Is there a reason why you stopped by?"

"Yes. I wanted to apologize for last night." He crossed the empty room to her. "I overstepped, asking you to talk to Billy in the first place. It's just that sometimes, I need to grasp at any possibility."

She frowned. "Does that mean that you're giving up on this?"

He shook his head. "No, I'll just find another way. I've been putting it off, but it's time I went through my father's things. I had years ago, but maybe I missed something."

Reed knew he should leave, work was waiting back in his office. But he'd always enjoyed being with Paige, talking with her. That hadn't changed. "Well, I should get going." He backed away, then turned around and headed for the stairs.

"Reed."

He stopped and looked over his shoulder.

"I could help you go over Mick's things if you want."

His day just got brighter. "I'd like that. I'll give you a call." He paused. "This means a lot to me, Paige."

"I want to help you find the truth."

Reed couldn't stop himself. He crossed the

room and drew her into his arms. She was resistant at first, but her body yielded into his. Reveling in her softness, he tightened his arms around her back, drawing her closer, alerting him to the increased fullness of her breasts pressed against his chest, the slight mound of her stomach. He tried to relax, to ignore his desire for her.

He'd have to be dead to do that.

Two nights later, Paige returned to the Larkin home. This time was different since Jodi wouldn't be around to act as chaperone. They would be alone.

Not a big deal. Reed was a friend and she was only here to help him. And even if she admitted that she still cared about the man, he wouldn't want to get involved with a pregnant woman. She didn't need another complication right now, she kept chanting as she climbed the porch steps. What worried her more was that he'd learn the truth about why she broke up with him after high school. He'd never forgive her for lying. She still needed to help her friend.

Suddenly the front door opened and Reed appeared. Wearing low riding jeans and a black polo shirt, he looked sexy with his dark, bedroom eyes and black wavy hair falling over his forehead. He smiled and her heart lodged in her throat.

The man had complication written all over him.

"You're just in time," he said, took her hand and pulled her inside.

"In time for what?"

"Pizza." He led her to the dining room where there were two places set at the corner of the table. "It's just coming out of the oven." He disappeared into the kitchen.

"You don't have to feed me," she called to

him, realizing she was hungry. "Did you make your homemade pizza?"

Reed returned with the round pie. "Is there any other kind?"

"It was all we had since there wasn't a pizzeria in town." His first attempts at making pizza hadn't been too successful. But they had had so much fun experimenting.

He ignored her as he cut her a slice and placed it on her plate. He nodded to her to sit. "Eat, it's got all the things you like."

"I hope your skills have improved over the years." Paige glanced at the golden-brown cheese topped with pepperoni, mushrooms and peppers. All her favorites.

"It does look good." Her stomach growled as she sank into the chair. "I guess I could eat something."

Grinning, he sat down. "Good. And we can work while we eat." He took a big bite of his piece and chewed as he reached for a file. "I went through Dad's papers today. I don't think there's much. But Mick had kept some notes in date books." Reed pulled out several. "They mostly just log his hours in the mine."

"Your father had another mining job during the day, didn't he?" Paige asked.

"Yes, he only worked Mick's Dream evenings and weekends. I remember because he wasn't home much." Reed opened one of the booklets. "In here, he only stated the tunnel he worked and if any silver ore was found."

Paige had finished her wedge of pizza and reached for another. "Did your father ever find any silver?"

"He had little strikes, but it wasn't much and he'd always put the money back into the mine." Reed stared off into space. "There were nights I could hear my parents fighting over the money and all the time Dad put in at the mine. Mom hated it." Reed studied her for a moment. "I hated the town gossip the most.

Dad was hardworking, and the most honest man I'd ever known." He sighed. "I know he enjoyed talking about finding the motherlode, but he'd never steal from anyone."

Paige had heard the stories, too. She saw firsthand how they'd hurt Reed. "And you really think he found it."

His deep gaze locked on hers. "I'd bet my life on it. Dad told me himself. What I don't understand is why Billy and Dad fought about it. If it were the big strike, wouldn't there be enough money for them both?"

"Maybe Mick found out about the forged partnership papers. Or he could have told Billy about the strike to say he was going to pay him back the loan, and maybe Billy wanted a bigger share." Stuffed, Paige pushed her plate away. "What's sad is that Hutchinson may be the only one who knows the truth."

Reed stared at her for a long time, then glanced down at the glass in his hand. "For years, I thought because of what people said about my father might have been the reason you broke up with me."

"Oh, no, Reed, never."

Reed wanted to believe her. But it still ate at him. Why suddenly had Paige's feelings for him changed? How had she given up on them?

"I guess as a guy, I've wondered all sorts of things." He looked at her beautiful face. The face that he couldn't get out of his head for years. "Why, Paige? What did I do to make you stop loving me?"

Paige blinked in surprise. "Oh, Reed, we were so young. I guess I got scared…but I never stopped…" She stood. "I need to go."

Reed wasn't about to let her go, not when he was so close. He took hold of her arm and turned her toward him. "Can't you at least be honest with me, Paige?"

"It was so long ago, Reed. Why should it matter now?"

He touched her cheek. "It does to me. You've mattered to me… Even now."

"This isn't a good idea," she pleaded, but she didn't move away.

"Why, because I'm stirring up feelings that have never gone away…for either of us?" He drew her into his arms. "Because you still care about me."

Reed lowered his head and captured her mouth in a kiss that he'd been aching for far too long. He groaned as she wrapped her arms around his back and held on. His pulse raced and his gut tightcncd when his tongue swept into her mouth tasting her sweetness, her hunger. He broke off the kiss, and opened his eyes to see the mirrored desire in her whiskey-colored gaze.

He cupped her face. "You can't tell me there still isn't something between us. The need… the excitement…"

She shook her head. "We're both vulnerable

right now, Reed. We're both reaching out for…comfort."

"I don't think that's all. We were friends a long time, Paige. We could depend on each…trust each other."

She missed that the most when she lost Reed. Their friendship. "Then be my friend now, Reed, and I'll be yours. I have too much on my plate right now to take it past that…for now anyway."

He grinned. "Can friends still kiss?"

Paige couldn't help but laugh and it felt good. Before she could answer her cell phone rang. She dug into her purse and answered it. She walked away for the conversation.

Reed went to the windows and stared outside, frustrated with himself for nearly blowing it. The last thing Paige needed was him acting like a randy teenager. She wasn't ready for him…for any man in that way. He'd give her time, but he wasn't going to let her always push him away forever.

Paige hung up. "I'd better go."

"Problems?" Reed asked.

"Morgan has a meeting tomorrow that she can't reschedule. She was going with me in the morning to get my things in Denver. We'll have to postpone until later in the week."

"No, you won't. I'll drive you."

"I can't ask you to do that." She swung her purse over her shoulder.

"You didn't, I offered," he argued. "I have a truck with a large bed in back. And as you already know I can carry heavy boxes— which you cannot. So you better get a good night's sleep because we have an early start in the morning." He gave her a gentle nudge toward the door, but Paige dug in her heels.

"You can't just take the day off."

He folded his arms across his chest. "I happen to have tomorrow off." He didn't, but had no doubt that one of his deputies would cover for him. "Besides, moving is a big job." His gaze narrowed while he waited for her to argue.

"And you happen to have strong muscles."

"Do you have a problem with that?" When she didn't say anything, he announced, "I'll pick you up at 5:00 a.m. Unless that's too early."

She stared at him a few seconds. "Anyone ever tell you, Larkin, you're bossy?"

"Only when I have to be." He kissed the end of her nose. "Now, go home and get to bed."

She glared. "Oh, I'm going to work you so hard tomorrow and you'll be sorry you volunteered."

He smiled as he watched her march out of the house. Never. He got to spend the day with her.

And that was a start.

CHAPTER SIX

THE next morning, Paige slept off and on during the long drive to Denver. Even though Reed's truck was a crew cab, she felt his constant presence, and kept inhaling the clean scent that was so uniquely his. That seemed to arouse a strong desire within her. She had the urge to lay her head against his shoulder and let him take care of it all.

No, she couldn't do that. This was her life, her new start, and she couldn't depend on another man. She had to do it on her own.

Finally Reed pulled off the interstate and Paige directed him to her neighborhood. To the place she'd called home for the past four years.

Although she'd only been gone three weeks, it seemed a lot longer. There had been so many changes in her life, and there were more to come. A new home, a new career and a whole new life all waiting back in Destiny.

Reed pulled into her parking space and shut off the engine. "We made it."

She looked toward her two-story town house. She loved this place. When she got her job with the D.A.'s office, it had marked her independence, and the beginnings of a successful career.

"It seems strange to be back here," she said.

"If you want, we can go have coffee and return later," Reed suggested.

As much as Paige wanted to run away, she knew it was just postponing the inevitable. "That's not going to help. We better get started."

They went up the walkway and Paige inserted the key, then opened the door. Inside was a small entry that led to a living room with a fireplace. A bar with two stools faced a galley-style kitchen with maple cabinets and biscuit-colored tiled countertops. She was suddenly flooded with memories of Drew and her sharing the crowded space as they prepared meals together.

Paige turned away. "If you'll bring in the boxes from the truck, I'll start cleaning out the bathroom cabinets."

When Reed returned, Paige had him pack up dishes in the kitchen and she moved into the bedroom and cleaned out the closets. They were quickly filling up boxes and Reed loaded them in the truck. What she didn't need for her new apartment, she boxed and put in the storage unit over her parking space.

Reed checked his watch. "I don't know about you but I'm running on empty. Are you hungry?"

Paige blinked. "You mean I have to feed you, too?"

He smiled. "I'd say that was pretty reasonable for free labor."

Once again Paige noticed how good-looking the man was when he smiled...or when he frowned...or when he just stood there. "I guess I don't mind paying for your muscle."

"So you've noticed." He flexed his arms.

She fought a blush and lost. She would have to be dead not to notice. "I had to make sure you could do the job."

He stepped closer. "How am I doing so far?"

"I'll let you know when the work is done."

"Okay, but we both need a break. I'll go and get us some food, and you can keep working if you want."

Paige gave him her order and while he was gone, she called to have her utilities shut off on Monday. Her new tenant had already arranged to have hers turned on before moving in.

Paige leaned back on the bar stool. Everything was just about finished. The truck was nearly packed. All the big pieces of furniture were staying in the condo. It was cheaper to buy new than pay for a moving van.

Maybe that was a good thing. Starting from scratch, with no memories of her life here. No chances of running into Drew.

Suddenly the phone rang and Paige jumped. She reached inside her purse thinking it was Reed and he'd gotten lost.

"So you can't find your way back," she said.

"Paige…"

She tensed, immediately recognizing the voice. "Drew…" She swallowed to clear her throat. "We don't have anything left to say."

"Oh, I think we do," he argued. "I waited to call until your new…boyfriend left. You work fast, Paige."

She stiffened. How dare he? "What do you want, Drew?"

"I just want to know what you're doing back here. You said you weren't coming back."

Was the man watching her? Suddenly feeling exposed, she got up and moved away from the windows. "When you walked out of my life two months ago you lost all rights. I'm not your concern."

"The hell you're not. And if you're here to cause trouble— You still pregnant?"

She wanted so badly to lie. "I am."

He cursed. "I warned you not to cause any trouble with my marriage."

If she'd had any leftover love for this man, it had just died. "The only thing I want from you, Drew, is to sign over to me all rights to this child."

"Only if you stay the hell out of my life."

"Gladly." Angry tears threatened, blinding her, but in reality she'd never seen more clearly than right now. "I'll get back you as to the time and place."

"This kid probably isn't even mine."

Another stab at her. "Think whatever you want, but this is a two-way street. I want you out of my, and my baby's, life."

"Maybe I'll just keep an eye on you to make sure you uphold your part of the deal."

He was watching her condo. "You stay away from me—"

Suddenly the phone was grabbed away. She swung around to see Reed place the receiver next to his ear. "I take it this is Detective Drew McCarran of Denver PD."

Reed paused. "Where I get my info is my business. And I'm sure there is much more on you, McCarran. I worked for the FBI for many years, and still have a lot of friends at the Bureau. If Paige says to stay out of her life, all you ask is how far away."

Reed listened, then laughed sarcastically.

"Believe me, Detective, I can make more trouble for you than you can for us. So my suggestion is you do exactly what Paige wants and we'll get along fine." He nodded. "Good, now that we understand each other, I'm going to end this conversation." He flipped the phone shut and dropped it on the counter along with the sacks of food.

Reed wanted to break something. Instead he paced the kitchen, trying to calm down. Talking to that jerk made him angrier than he'd been in a long time. But when it came to Paige, he would protect her at all costs.

"Do you really have people at the Bureau who could hurt Drew?"

He shrugged. "I still have friends. And as a rule scumbags like McCarran have things in their past they don't want to come out... I haven't dug that deep...yet."

"I don't want you to do anything. I just want him gone from my life." She brushed a tear off her cheek. "I can't believe I was so naïve to get involved with him," she whispered. "Oh God, I'm so ashamed."

Reed was right there taking her into his arms. "Shh, Paige. It's not your fault the man lied to you. You trusted that he'd care about you."

"It's not that, it's me." She pulled away. "I'm ashamed that I don't feel anything for Drew. And he's the father of my child."

"No, he's the sperm donor. There's a difference. The man doesn't deserve to be a father, or he'd stand by you."

Reed made her look at him, hoping she saw how he felt about her. How he'd always felt about her.

"As for your falling for the guy, we've all needed someone to be there." His voice grew husky. "Sometimes it might not be the person we want it to be, but we want love so badly…want someone to love us just because we're so tired of being alone."

Paige swallowed, then whispered, "Was there someone special?"

Trish Davidson's face flashed in Reed's head as he nodded. "Trish was my partner at the Bureau. We worked together on a lot of assignments. It seemed natural, and in life-and-death situations, you grasp at the living part."

"Is…is she the reason you left the FBI?"

"Partly. Trish died," he said and she gasped.

Reed had to keep talking…he had to get the story out. "I second-guessed my actions that night, wondering if there was something I could have done to save her." He glanced down at the compassion in Paige's eyes. "So see we all carry around baggage, a lot of wrong choices and a lot of regrets."

"I'm sorry, Reed."

He nodded. "When Mom had her stroke I made the decision to come back to Destiny. It was time. Time to stop running away…to face things." He sighed. "But it's hard when the past has a hold on you."

She reached up and touched his jaw. "And you've been hurt, Reed. It's hard to let go. I'm not doing so well, either."

He might have moved on with his career, but his dad's disappearance still haunted him. "You will."

"It frightens me sometimes." She pulled away and stroked her stomach protectively. "Starting up a new law practice, and having a baby is a little frightening."

"I have no doubt you can do it. Besides, you have your family around to help you."

"They've been great." She gave him a hint of a smile. "And so have you."

This time Reed couldn't stop himself as he placed his hand over hers. "I've wanted to be there for you, too."

She smiled. "Be careful what you promise. I may just take you up on it."

His heart was beating so hard, he thought she could hear it. "I care about you, Paige, and your baby. Would it be so bad for you to depend on me a little?"

Paige swallowed. It would be so easy, but they had too much in the past. Too much to keep them from having a future together. "If things were different maybe I would take you up on it."

Reed reached for her. "There's nothing I see that's stopping us," he said as he lowered his mouth to hers.

It was a gentle kiss, but it didn't lack impact as he slowly, pleasurably, persuaded her into a response. Coaxing her lips apart, he slipped inside to taste her. She whimpered as his sure hands roamed over her back, cradling her against his strong body, making her feel both protected and needy. By the time he finally released her, she wanted to cry in protest. "Oh, Reed…"

"I think I made my point," he told her, then

winked. He directed her to a chair at the counter where the food was. "Now, you'd better eat. I want you at full strength when I get down to some serious convincing about us being together."

Paige decided not to protest now. Later, she would set Reed straight about them.

Just as soon as she figured out what that was.

A week later, the honeymoon couple returned home and invited everyone for a get-together at the Silver R Ranch. The late-summer evening was perfect for an outdoor barbecue.

Even though Paige was busy setting up her office, she was eager to see Leah, and she admitted to herself, Reed, too.

It hadn't taken much encouragement for her family to include Reed in their gathering, especially after all the attention he'd shown Paige.

The memory of their trip to Denver, and Reed's kiss still had her reeling. But that had been the last one. He hadn't been by her office to check on her, or even at her parents' Inn. Over the past week she'd only caught glimpses of him in his patrol car around town. He'd tossed her a wave, but that was as close as she'd gotten. It was good that he'd got on with his life, and she could live hers.

Paige turned off the highway and the ranch house came into view. Seeing the familiar black truck, her pulse began to race. She told herself she was excited to see her sister, but she knew Reed had been the big draw.

She got out and reached in back to pull out a large Queen Elizabeth rosebush she'd bought as a housewarming present and headed for the deck out back. Hearing the laughter, she quickened her steps. Since moving out of her parents' a few days ago, she realized just how much she'd missed her family.

Paige turned the corner and saw Reed right off, drinking a tall glass of iced tea. He probably had to go on patrol later.

Leah and Holt were wrapped in a loving embrace. Their smiling nine-year-old son, Corey, standing close by. No doubt he was happy that his parents were back home.

"I heard the world traveler was back in town."

Leah broke away and ran to greet her. "Paige," she cried as she hugged her, ignoring the rosebush. "How are you feeling?"

Paige laughed. "I'm feeling good, but you're smashing your welcome home gift."

Leah released her, but her smile held fast. "Oh, it's beautiful. Is it guaranteed not to die?" Holt appeared at her side and slipped a protective arm around her. The couple exchanged a look that seemed to heat the air between them. Paige glanced toward the deck to find Reed watching her.

"Honey, look what Paige brought us."

Never taking his eyes from his wife, he said, "It's beautiful, Paige. Thank you."

Paige smiled. "You're welcome. I'd ask how the honeymoon went, but I can see you both had a wonderful time."

"Hawaii was incredible," Leah gushed. "We swam and snorkeled and we walked on the beach…caught every beautiful sunset…" Leah turned to Holt as a blush rose across her cheeks. "And sunrises…"

"For someone who had spent the last four years traveling the world," her new husband said, "you seemed pretty captivated by the Hawaiian Islands."

Leah looked up at Holt. "I guess it was the company, and your persuasive ways." She leaned closer and whispered something that Paige didn't want to hear.

"I think I'll go say hi to Mom and Dad." She walked toward the back of the deck and hugged her parents.

"So how was your first night in your place?" her father asked.

"Just fine. I still have boxes to unpack but it's turning into home."

"If you change your mind, you know you can come back home," her mother said. "We could remodel your old room and…"

"Mom," Paige said warningly. "We talked about this. I've been on my own since college. And when the baby comes it won't be as disturbing, especially to the guests."

"This baby is our grandchild. We don't care who he or she disturbs." Claire finally smiled. "But your father and I understand your need your privacy and your own life. But we better be on the top of the list for baby-sitters."

"Oh, you definitely will be." She glanced at her older sister. "Morgan is running a close second."

Morgan walked over. "And I can't wait," she said. "I'm going to spoil her to death."

"Her!" Paige was feeling her own excitement. "Do you know something I don't?"

Morgan shrugged. "I just have a feeling it's going to be a girl. They do run in our family."

"I want a boy," Corey said.

"Well, it's going to be one or the other." Reed joined the group. "Hi, Paige. How are you?"

She could feel everyone's eyes on them. "I'm fine." *I've missed you,* she said silently. Who wouldn't?

Dressed in his usual jeans, with a dark green Henley shirt, he had on cowboy boots, making him even taller than his six foot one in height.

"Nearly all moved in," she said.

"Good," he said as his dark gaze made her too aware of him as a man…of his heated kisses, his slow, burning touches. And Reed Larkin was the last person she needed to be thinking about.

Somehow her parents had wandered off, leaving them alone. "Did you just get off-duty?"

"I'm going in later. I took Jodi and Nick out to see Mom today. Jodi and Mom both said hi."

"I should go see your mom." In truth, Paige hadn't wanted to go back to Shady Haven, but it had nothing to do with Sally Larkin.

"I could take you tomorrow." He lowered his voice. "Maybe you could talk with Billy again."

Paige didn't want to discuss this. "Can we talk about this later?"

He nodded. "I'll follow you back to your place."

Paige agreed, but she knew Reed wouldn't be happy with what she had to tell him, or her decision not to talk with Billy again.

It was after ten when Reed followed Paige into the alley behind her building. He parked his truck at the real estate office next door.

It had been a week since he'd been alone

with Paige. She asked for time and, although it had nearly killed him, he gave it to her.

He climbed out of the truck and walked over to help her out of the car and realized a light was out over the door. "You should call and have the light fixed. It's too dark out here."

"I guess I haven't noticed it." She slipped the key in the dead bolt and opened the door to the dimly lit hallway. Immediately she went to the alarm system and punched in the code.

"Good, you have an alarm."

"I'll have private files here." She smiled at him. "So if someone breaks in I can expect a fast response for law enforcement?"

He grinned, enjoying her easy mood. "I'm here to protect and serve."

"That's good to hear. Come on, I'll give you the nickel tour." She led him down the hall to the front of the building to the reception area. There was now a chocolate-brown sofa and two chairs, along with a glass-top coffee table arranged in the waiting area. A geometrical patterned rug covered the hardwood. On the other side was a desk.

"This is nice. Do you have a receptionist?"

"Just me until I build a client list." She then walked him into her office and turned on the light. The walls had been painted a slate-blue and floor-to-ceiling bookshelves were bright-white and the books were neatly organized. A dark red carpet felt plush under his feet.

He let out a low whistle. "Impressive."

"Thank you. That's what I was going for."

Paige stood across the room. All night she'd been careful not to get too close. "Does the upstairs look this good?"

"It's still bare bones. Give me another week to finish unpacking and buy some more furniture."

"That won't bother me. I bet you have a coffeemaker." He took her by the arm. "Make me a cup and we'll talk."

Paige didn't like the way Reed took over, but she allowed him to escort her upstairs to where there was a rust print love seat and a maple table and four chairs from her parents' Inn. A new mahogany bedroom set had been delivered only yesterday. "I'm still unpacking all the stuff we brought back from Denver." She was nervous of what he thought of the place.

He walked around. "Seems you have all the essentials."

"Typical man. Women like a little more decor." She went to the windows that she'd come to love. Morgan had made her Roman shades for privacy, and she could still enjoy the sunlight. "I need to concentrate on buying baby furniture." She went in the kitchen area, reached for a stainless steel canister and began scooping coffee into the coffeemaker. "Mom has a lot of things left over from Leah, but I suspect my sister will want a baby soon. So I decided to buy new."

Reed glanced at her slightly protruding stomach. For the average person Paige didn't show, but he'd felt the baby growing inside her. He'd noticed subtle changes in her body. She had a beautiful glow. "You're in the second trimester."

She paused from her task and glanced over her shoulder. She nodded. "Sixteen weeks."

"I only know because I've lived through this with Jodi. I think she read every pregnancy book to me."

"It's nice that you could be there for her."

The realization of his need to be there for Paige tore at him. But first, she needed to clear her life of her past. He did, too. "I know you've been busy trying to get your practice going, but I need you to talk to Billy again."

Paige carried two mugs to the table. "I hope you don't mind decaf. It's all I have."

Reed crossed the room. "Paige, I don't care

about the damn coffee, I need to know if you're going to talk to Billy again."

Paige sat down at the table. "No, Reed, I'm not."

CHAPTER SEVEN

REED got off work at 6:00 a.m. and headed out of town, driving a little faster than the speed limit. He needed to clear his head of everything, especially of the woman who'd been crowding into his thoughts 24/7.

His other constant distraction was Billy Hutchinson. The old man talking about his father's disappearance had Reed more determined than ever to find out the truth. Damn, he felt so close to some news about his father.

For too many years, he hadn't been able to clear his family's name. He'd kept running into dead ends. And now, he finally thought he had a slim chance with Billy, but Paige refused to help him.

Once again she'd let him down.

Reed reached the highway turnoff to the mine and started up the dirt road. Shifting into four-wheel drive, he started up the rough incline. Tall pines lined the winding route and huge chiseled boulders stood out along the foothills, marking the way toward his destination. Mick's Dream.

Memories of his dad bringing him here flooded his head. Happy memories. Ones he'd never forget. And more than ever, they'd never be tarnished by what other people thought or said.

Reed drove over the rise and pulled his truck into a flat area under the tall pines only to discover another truck already parked there. To be on the side of caution, he took his sidearm out of the glove compartment and climbed out. Strapping on his gun, he headed up the gravel-like grade toward the mine. Someone was trespassing on private property. His property.

Reed hadn't been here in years. Not since the day he'd left town for college. Then the place had been boarded up under Billy's orders, supposedly because it wasn't safe. With his father not around, his mother hadn't argued Hutchinson's decision. She'd only wanted the ugly rumors of her husband being a thief to die down.

Reed had been just a kid then, but old enough to know that the sheriff back then had done very little, if anything, to aid in the search for Mick. What could Reed expect? Sheriff Don McGriff was one of Billy's "good old boy" buddies. Well, he was the sheriff now, and this was still Larkin property.

Reed stopped about twenty feet from the entrance when he saw the fencing materials. Two men came out of the mine and were carrying tools. He had a feeling Lyle Hutchinson had a hand in this.

He rested his hand on his gun. "Stop where you are."

Both men froze.

Reed didn't give them a chance to speak. "You're trespassing on private property," he stated, resting his hand on his gun belt. "I'm Sheriff Larkin. State your business here."

"Hey, Sheriff," one of the middle-aged men spoke up. "We're just doing the job we were paid for."

"Like I said, this is private property."

"We got permission from the owner."

"Doubt that since I'm the owner. Who sent you?"

The two exchanged another confused look. "Lyle Hutchinson hired us to board up the mine…permanently. He wanted to make sure it was secure…make sure that kids wouldn't get inside. So we're fencing the area."

Reed couldn't argue that it would be the safest thing to do. Too many foolish people were killed in abandoned mines. But it seemed strange that, after all these years, Hutchinson had decided to do it now.

"Okay, finish the job you were hired for, just make sure you drop off a key to the gate at my office." With their nod, Reed turned and walked away. He was finished giving Hutchinsons all the control. And maybe it was time he let Lyle know that.

Two hours later Reed arrived at his house to find Paige's car in the driveway. She was waiting on the porch. He wasn't ready to face her now, but it didn't look like he had a choice.

He climbed out of the truck and walked toward the house. She stood up as he approached.

She looked tired and sad, still nothing took

away from her appeal. And nothing would stop the ache he felt for her, or the need to pull her into his arms, and bury himself in her softness.

He fought his feelings. "You're up early."

Paige brushed back a strand of hair and took a deep breath, trying to relax. She hated the edgy nervous feeling Reed caused in her. "I didn't sleep very well." Her gaze searched his. "I couldn't stop thinking about you.…"

He tensed, but gave her a careless shrug. "Why? You said it all last night." He brushed by her and opened his front door, then paused to look back at her. "Or did you? Is there something else, Paige?"

"Yes…"

He stood back and motioned for her to go inside. Paige knew that things were going to change drastically if she walked through that door. She had no choice. No matter what, she had to do what was right. She squeezed by him and went into the living room.

"I don't have any decaf," he said. "Jodi left some tea. Would you like a cup?"

She shook her head. "I just came to say, I'm sorry…and if you want me to talk with Billy, I will." She fought to keep the tremor from her voice. "Just let me know when you want to go. Goodbye, Reed." She made it to the door and pulled it open when she felt his hand on her arm.

"What made you change your mind?" he asked, so close to her she could feel his breath against her cheek.

Paige looked up at him and was caught by his mesmerizing gaze. Her pulse shot off. "It's the right thing to do. I know you might not believe me, but I've always wanted to help you."

"And I appreciate that, Paige."

She nodded and turned to business. "Now, I'm no expert, but whatever happened that night between the two men, I have a feeling Billy has remorse, is looking for some forgiveness. And you might be the person to get him to confess."

Reed remained silent as if contemplating her words, then said, "So you'll go with me?"

She nodded. "It still isn't a good idea." Paige was also worried about what else Billy would say about her part in getting Reed to leave town. "I should stay out of this."

Reed raised his hand to her cheek. His touch was warm, and stirred feelings she didn't want to analyze.

"I want you with me, Paige. I've always needed you." He leaned down and placed a soft kiss on her cheek, then moved to the other side and repeated the action.

"Oh, Reed… This isn't a good idea."

He kissed her eyelids. "You and me together is the best idea."

She had trouble breathing. She wanted so badly to believe him, to push aside the past. "It's not just you and me. My baby."

Reed pulled back slightly and stared down at her. "You think I don't care about your baby? He or she is part of you, Paige, how could I not care?" He placed a hand against her stomach and his mouth covered hers in a soft kiss. "Do you want me to show you?"

Paige wanted to give in. Suddenly she heard footsteps on the porch. They jumped back to find Lyle Hutchinson standing there, smiling. "Well, what do we have here?"

Lyle was in his mid-fifties. Tall, slender and still a nice-looking man with thick gray hair, he was dressed in a tailor-made dark suit. He came from the first family of Destiny and had always tried to use that to his advantage.

"What are you doing here, Hutchinson?" Reed asked, holding Paige close.

"Since you threatened my crew, Larkin, I think it's time we got together. Besides, you'll want to hear what I have to say." Lyle glanced at Paige. "And maybe it's a good idea if your…lawyer is present to witness this. Then maybe we can get out of each other's lives once and for all."

When Reed opened the door to allow the man inside, Paige had a feeling that this wasn't going to end things. It was just the beginning.

The meeting took place at the dining room table, but Reed wasn't offering any welcoming gestures. He wanted to just get down to business. Lyle came prepared as he opened his briefcase, pulled out a paper and pushed it across the highly polished wood.

"What's this?" Reed asked, hating to be caught off guard.

"It's an official offer to buy out your family's shares in Mick's Dream. It's a fair offer, Reed. Probably more than it's worth."

What was going on? Reed read over the agreement that stated the mine was going to be closed permanently. Of course, the Larkin family didn't have any money to start up a mining operation anyway.

"Why now, Lyle? Why do you suddenly want to buy me out?"

Hutchinson didn't give anything away in his expression. "I'm just trying to clean up some loose ends. You have to admit that this mine is like a dark cloud over all our lives. There are no good memories of the place." He nodded to the paper. "This money should help with your mother's care."

That infuriated Reed. The Hutchinsons had never cared about Sally Larkin. "Leave my mother out of this. If your family had cared about my family, Billy would have never spread lies about Mick."

Lyle stiffened. "My offer is more than generous, but read the fine print. The offer's not going to be on the table forever." He shut his briefcase. "Think about it, Larkin. For everyone's sake." He headed for the door and walked out.

Reed looked at Paige reading over the agreement.

She blew out a breath. "This is a lot of money."

He only stared at her, then asked, "Is this the lawyer talking or my…friend?"

Paige studied him a moment. "As a lawyer, I'd say this would insure you and your family a lot of security, but I know you, Reed. You want to find out what happened to your father." Her eyes were pleading. "My concern is, what if that never happens?"

"I know it might backfire in my face, but I can't just walk away." His throat was suddenly thick with emotion. "I've got to try."

A half smile appeared on her pretty face. "That's what I expected you'd say," she said. "If you want I'll go with you to see Billy. But you know if Lyle gets wind of this, he'll do everything he can to keep you away from his father."

"I know I can't use anything Billy has to say in court. I guess at this point I just need to learn anything that will tell me what happened to my dad. If Billy can lead me in the right direction I've got to go there."

"Even if that direction doesn't have a good end?"

Reed wasn't foolish enough to think his father was still alive. "You mean finding my father dead."

Paige shook her head. "I mean, not being able to make the guilty pay."

It was two days before Reed had a chance to go to Shady Haven. Over the weekend Jodi had visited while he had to fill in the shifts of his sick deputy. Today he was off, and he'd come out early to spend time with his mother, and show her Lyle's offer to buy the mine.

Reed knew that Sally Larkin's stroke had taken a physical toll, but there was nothing wrong with her mental faculties. He handed her the paper assuming that she'd want him to take the money for their future and little Nicky.

Reed wasn't worried about his financial future. He'd been paid well at the Bureau, and he'd invested wisely over the years. Even managed to send some money home. So Lyle's offer wasn't of any interest to him. It only told him that Hutchinson was guilty of something. And he was going to find out what.

"A lot of…money," Sally told him.

"We don't need it. I can take care of you," he said. "And Jodi."

Sally's clear blue eyes were kind and loving. She shook her head. "Mick's Dream… is trouble."

"I know, Mother. But I need to know what happened that night. Billy has said things that lead me to believe he lied about Dad."

She touched his hand. "Yes. Mick d…did not steal."

"I know, Mom. I'm going to clear Dad's name. Paige is going to help me."

Sally Larkin's smile was slightly crooked from the stroke. "You and Paige. Nice…"

"That was a long time ago, Mom. It's different now."

"She still…cares."

Reed wanted to believe that, but he was afraid to hope.

"Paige is pregnant," he said.

His mother nodded. "Claire s…said." She studied him. "B…baby bother you?"

He could lie and say he didn't wish the child was his. "It's part of Paige." He stood. It was strange he was talking to his mother about this. "I don't care for the jerk she was involved with."

His mother's eyes and smile told him she wanted the two of them to be together. He wanted the same, but he couldn't think about that now. He kissed her cheek. "I've got to go. I'll stop by tomorrow. Love ya, Mom."

"L…love you."

Reed walked out the door. He probably was a fool to get involved with Paige. He couldn't seem to help it. Who was to say that McCarran wouldn't call her and say he wanted Paige back. Worse, what if she went running?

Reed reached the sitting area at the home and looked around. As usual, he found Billy seated at the wide doors, but this day he wasn't alone. Lyle was with him. He quickly turned and headed out the door. The last thing he wanted was for either man to see him. But he wasn't going to let Billy off the hook. He would find out the truth, one way or the other.

"The baby, at week sixteen, is four to five inches long, and weighs a bit less than three ounces," Morgan recited as they walked quickly around the park. "He or she can make a fist." Paige's sister grinned but kept her arms pumping as they walked briskly around Town Square Park. "Isn't it wonderful?"

"She sure feels more than three ounces pressed against my bladder." Paige had read all this herself, but Morgan was getting a kick out of being a source of information.

"We can stop if you have to go," Morgan said.

"No, I think I can make it back to the office." Her sister had decided that exercise was a good idea for the both of them. So she'd started walking in the afternoons if her schedule allowed it.

The fresh air and increased heart rate seemed to be helping with her stress levels and her increased appetite. She had a doctor's appointment in two weeks and didn't want the scale to become her enemy at this early stage.

When they turned and cut across the grassy playground, she saw Reed ahead, walking out of the sheriff's office. She allowed herself the luxury of giving the sexy lawman the once-over. He must do his own workout to stay in such good shape and look that great. The tailored uniform shirt tapered over his broad shoulders and narrow waist. Oh, boy. Her body heated up and she doubted it was from the brisk walk.

As if he sensed something, he suddenly looked in her direction. His mirrored sunglasses hid his expression as he raised a hand and gave them a friendly wave.

She waved back just as she felt her ankle buckle and give way on the uneven ground. She gasped as she collapsed and fell to her knees.

"Paige," Morgan cried and rushed to her aid. "Are you okay?"

Paige was embarrassed more than anything, but there was pain, too. "I twisted my ankle." She sat down on the grass just as Reed appeared at her side. Several other Destiny residents made an appearance.

"Don't move," he insisted. "Where do you hurt?"

"My ankle." She released her hold on the pained area and he took over the examination. His large, sure hands were gentle as he tested her injury.

"Really, I'm okay, I just stepped in a hole."

"Do you hurt anywhere else?" His concerned gaze met hers. "What about the baby?"

She shook her head. "I caught myself with my hands."

"You sure?"

Suddenly Paige realized how serious this could be and was angry she let herself get distracted. "Yes, but I feel stupid for not watching where I was going."

One corner of his mouth twitched. "It happens to the best of us."

She glanced around at the crowd. "Seems I'm drawing attention."

He stood. "Okay, everyone, Paige is fine. She just twisted her ankle."

As people moved on, Reed was back at her side.

"Boy, you're good at crowd control."

"I scored high on my Bureau test."

Morgan leaned over. "I think we should take you to the emergency room to have your ankle looked at."

Paige wasn't going to argue, not until Reed scooped her up unto his arms. "Wait," she gasped, but wrapped her arms around his neck when he started off across the park. It was like a scene out of a movie. Instead she was being carried off by a real-life hero. "Reed, this isn't necessary," she said weakly, too aware of the man holding her.

"It's the fastest way to get you to my car."

Morgan trailed behind them. "Just enjoy it, Paige. You're seeing Destiny's finest at work."

They made it to the patrol car, and Morgan

hurried ahead to open the passenger door. "I'll get your purse and follow you there in my own car."

Paige grabbed her sister's arm. "Promise me you won't call Mom and Dad until we hear what the doctor has to say."

"I won't, but you have to call them, Paige," Morgan insisted.

She watched as Reed went around to the driver's side. "Okay, I will, after I see the doctor."

With that agreement Morgan took off and Reed climbed in the car. First, he radiocd thc office to let them know where he was going, then he started the engine.

Before he could pull away from the curb, Paige grabbed him by the arm. "You turn on your siren, Larkin, and you're dead meat."

He cocked an eyebrow, looking sexy and dangerous. "Oh, threatening an officer, that's a serious offence."

"I mean it."

"Okay, you got a reprieve." His mouth twitched. "Now, what have you got for me?"

She suddenly blushed as her thoughts only came up with things that were X-rated. "You get my undying gratitude."

Reed nodded slowly, the humor gone from his intense gaze. "Is that all you have to offer?"

The heat only intensified between them. "Take it or leave it."

"I'll take time with you anyway I can get it."

Two hours later, Paige had had her ankle X-rayed and wrapped after the doctor told her it was a sprain.

Something she already knew. Next came the call to her mother.

"No, Mom, I'm fine. And the baby is fine, too." Paige tried to convince her, but she still wanted to talk to Morgan.

With her crutch under her arm and the assurance she'd stay off her ankle for today, Paige made her way to the reception area where she found Reed waiting for her. Her heart soared as he leaned against the counter. His uniform was gone, replaced by a navy-blue polo shirt and jeans. He spotted her and came to help.

"Please, I can walk by myself," she said.

He frowned. "I take it everything is all right?"

"Yes, it is, and that includes the baby." She was relieved, too. "I do have to go see Dr. York tomorrow."

"I'll drive you."

She glared at him. She didn't want to keep leaning on him. She didn't want to get used to it and then lose him again. "I can do this, Reed. I can't keep taking you away from your job."

"I'm off tomorrow."

Morgan appeared at her side. "Mom said

you were to come home for dinner." She smiled at Reed. "All of us, Sheriff."

"I don't want to intrude," Reed said.

"Mom's made pot roast and garlic mashed potatoes."

"Keep talking…"

"Banana cream pie."

He groaned. "How can I turn that down?" He backed away. "I'll bring the car around." He disappeared through the doors.

Morgan cleared her throat. "He was pretty worried when you fell."

Paige countered. "I don't want him to worry."

"Whether you do or not, he does." Morgan sighed. "Paige, just because you got tangled up with a jerk doesn't mean all guys are like him. Reed has proved to be one the good guys."

"I just don't have the energy to start a relationship right now. I have a child to think about."

Her sister nodded. "I have a feeling that Reed would wait as long as it took."

Paige wanted to believe that. How easy it would be to depend on a man like Reed. But he wasn't hers anymore. Although years had passed, would he understand why she had to break up with him back then? Would he believe it was for his own good?

"Mrs. K, dinner was delicious," Reed said as he pushed his pie plate away. "Thank you for inviting me."

"You're always welcome here. Anytime."

"Thank you," he said. Paige's mother had always treated him like family. "It's nice to have the company, too."

"And you don't always eat well when you're alone." Claire Keenan's gaze went to Paige. "It's hard to cook for one."

"Mother, I eat just fine," Paige said as she tried to stand.

Reed relieved her of her plate. "Don't even think about it. You were told to stay off your ankle. Morgan and I can handle a few dishes."

Reed didn't want Paige to do a thing. He'd been frightened out of ten years of his life today. He never wanted to go through that again. He knew from experience that pregnant women weren't that fragile, but he worried that Paige was trying to do too much.

Morgan was at the sink rinsing dishes to go in the dishwasher. "Thank you for the help—and for today, too."

"Anytime."

"I do have another favor to ask you," Morgan hedged. "I have this conference call tomorrow. And Paige has a doctor's appointment at one... She doesn't want Mom and Dad to know she's going—so they won't worry. She shouldn't drive herself..."

"I can take her." Reed knew that it would be a problem, but only for Paige.

"She'll argue with you about it," Morgan countered.

"And I'll just argue right back. If I have to I'll carry her there."

Morgan smiled. "I knew I could depend on you."

Reed looked across the room at the woman in question.

Paige's soft pink blouse hung loosely over her rounded belly. In just days she seemed to have blossomed with her pregnancy. His gaze moved to her face and their eyes locked. Just one look from her and his body stirred to life. He glanced away.

"I want Paige to know she can depend on me, too."

The next afternoon Paige was wearing a paper gown and covered by a paper blanket, sitting on a paper-protected exam table. But she didn't care. Although Dr. York believed that the baby had not been affected by her fall yesterday, she was going to do an ultrasound.

Paige hadn't expected to have the procedure done for another two weeks.

There was a knock on the door and Dr. York peered in. She smiled. "Okay, Paige." She walked to the table. "You ready to see your baby?"

Nodding, Paige felt the tears well in her eyes. She suddenly wished she'd told her mother and asked her to come with her. This was a time when she didn't want to be alone. She nodded. "I'm nervous. You're sure there isn't anything wrong with the baby?"

The pretty, dark-haired doctor raised an eyebrow. "As I told you in my office, Paige, this is only a precaution."

"Okay." She just didn't want to face this alone. "Is Reed still here?"

Without saying a word, Dr. York went to the door and stepped outside. In seconds, Reed appeared in the room. He walked to her side and took her hand. "Are you okay?"

She released a long breath, flashing back to years before, recalling that he'd been her friend. "Would you look at my baby with me?"

A slow grin spread across his handsome face. "I'd love to." He leaned down and placed a soft kiss on her mouth. "It's going to be okay, Paige. I promise. Just hang on to me."

The doctor returned. "Well, ready to go?"

Paige nodded.

Reed moved out of the way, but refused to release Paige's hand. He also found he was nervous when the doctor lowered the sheet, exposing Paige's slightly rounded stomach. Emotions clogged his throat and he had to work hard just to swallow. She looked so beautiful.

The doctor took a tube of lubricant and spread some on Paige's stomach. "Sorry, it's a little cold." She placed a probe on her belly, then did some adjusting on the machine. Soon a rhythmic sound filled the room. The doctor smiled. "I just love the sound of a healthy heartbeat."

"That's the baby's…?" Paige breathed.

"That's your baby's heartbeat. It's steady and strong." The doctor shifted the probe. "Now, let's try to get a look at this kid."

Seconds ticked by until finally the picture on the screen began to come into focus. "There you are," Dr. York said as she pointed to the image. "See, there's the outline of the head, the spine…"

"I see it," Paige gasped. "Do you see her, Reed?"

He saw the tiny shadowed image. "I see her."

The doctor smiled. "So you think it's a girl?"

"My sister Morgan is convinced it is," Paige admitted.

"Well, it's a little early, but I might be able to learn the sex." The doctor continued to slide the probe over Paige's belly, then stopped. "Bingo." She turned to Paige. "Do you want to know?"

Paige glanced up at Reed. "Do we?"

Reed stared at her golden-whiskey colored gaze. He was so close to losing it, it wasn't funny. The intimacy between them at this moment was like nothing he'd ever felt with anyone.

"Of course you do. Whenever could you wait for anything?" he teased. But what he was sharing with this woman wasn't a joke. He was so crazy about her…and her baby. "At the very least, you'll know what color to paint the nursery."

Paige fought a smile. "More likely who I'm going to be sharing my room with."

Suddenly he envied this kid. He wanted to be her roommate…permanently. "Okay, Doctor, give us the news. Is it pink or blue?"

"It's a girl."

They grinned at each other. "Perfect."

CHAPTER EIGHT

IT'S a girl.

Paige was still smiling hours later when Reed drove her back to Destiny. She was having a little girl, and had the ultrasound pictures to prove it.

She'd been so happy over the news that her stumble in the park hadn't hurt the baby that nothing else mattered, until it finally hit her. She was going to be a mother.

Her joy had been so overwhelming she hadn't wanted to come down just yet. And Reed never questioned her when she'd asked to go to the mall where she'd spent the next few hours looking at cribs and baby clothes.

"I bet you're tired," Reed said. "It's been a long day for you and…Sweet Pea."

She looked across the cab at his handsome profile. "So you've already nicknamed her."

"Well, you have to admit, she isn't much bigger than a pea."

Paige liked it. "Oh, Reed, can you believe I'm having a girl?"

"The question is, is the world ready for a Paige Junior?"

"Can't handle a strong woman, huh, Larkin?"

"Strong I can deal with, but combined with stubborn, bullheaded and know-it-all types it's lethal."

"Oh, you poor baby," she cooed. She had no doubt that Reed Larkin could handle any woman, young or old. Over the years she'd fantasized about the boy she'd loved so desperately, and always hoped one day they'd somehow get back together. But she knew it could be too late for that.

Turning away, she studied the ultrasound printout. "I can't wait to show these pictures to Mom and Dad. I called home and Morgan said they went out to dinner with some friends."

"Did you tell your sister?"

Paige shook her head. "Just that everything went fine. I want to tell everyone together." She recalled how Reed had been there with her, holding her hand. "Reed...I want to thank you for coming with me today."

He gave her an easy smile, making her heart flutter. "I'm honored that you asked me." He turned off the highway and entered the town limits. "How about I drop you off at the apartment, then I'll pick up a pizza for dinner?"

Paige knew she shouldn't, but she didn't want this day to end, or her time with Reed. "You don't have anything better to do than hang around with a pregnant woman?"

He pulled up in front of her building.

"There's nothing I'd rather do. So I'll call in a pizza and be back in about twenty minutes."

She nodded. "I'll leave the door unlocked."

Reed pulled out his cell phone and began to dial the number before Paige was out of the truck. There was nothing wrong with sharing a pizza with a friend, she told herself, especially when that friend had given up his day to help her out.

Once inside the office, Paige listened to her phone messages. Two clients needed to reschedule their appointments. After she'd made the calls, and spent time to calm another client, she started toward the apartment when she heard a knock on the door. She walked through the reception area to see the familiar brown mail delivery truck. She pulled open the door and the driver handed her an envelope.

"I need a signature, ma'am," he said.

After scribbling down her name, she said goodbye and closed the door. She glanced at the sender to see a law firm in Denver. A sudden dread washed over her when she realized it was from Drew. She walked down the long hall to the back and made her way up the stairs to her apartment.

Dropping the envelope on the table, she went to the windows. This was her new sanctuary, the new home for her and her child. She'd added more and more personal touches each day. The bench had been covered in a cranberry and white toile print cushion, courtesy of her big sister, as was the beautiful quilt covering her bed.

Paige glanced back at the envelope. Why today? Why did he have to ruin today for her?

Well, she wasn't going to let him. She marched to the table and tore open the folder. Inside, she found several papers clipped together. She recognized the form immediately as the agreement she had sent to Drew at the first of last week.

The man couldn't even take the time to think about this life-changing decision. Paige scanned the papers and found his signature scribbled on the bottom line, and notarized by his attorney. She let out a long breath. That was it. Drew McCarran was out of her life… and his daughter's.

A tear found its way down her cheek when she realized her child was now fatherless.

"Paige…"

She looked up to see Reed standing at the top of the stairs. She tried to smile, but it didn't work. She sank into the chair and covered her face with her hands.

Reed set down the pizza box and rushed to her. He took the papers from her and glanced over them to find the familiar name on the bottom. Hell, the man's timing stank.

"I'm sorry, Paige," he whispered, but only meant it halfheartedly. He didn't want McCarran anywhere in her life.

"It's going to be okay." He drew her into his arms. She trembled against him, but refused to cry. "Let it go, babe. I'm here."

She pulled back, her expression sad. "How could I have been such a fool?"

"It's him, Paige, not you."

"But my baby… He doesn't even care about her." Her lip trembled as another tear found its way down her cheek. "She isn't even born yet…and she doesn't have a father."

Seeing the woman he cared about in pain nearly broke his heart. He pulled her back into his arms. "Hey, Sweet Pea will have something more important. She'll have people who truly love her. Your parents, Morgan, Leah…Holt and Corey…and me."

Would she let him love her and her child? "Would you let me in your life, Paige? Let me prove to you that all men aren't jerks?"

She sniffed and looked up at him. Her eyes

were red from crying and her makeup smeared. She was beautiful.

"How can you want that? All those years ago…I left you."

He stopped her words. "That was a long time ago. Things are different now. We're different. The only thing that's the same is how I feel about you, how I've always felt about you."

She stepped out of his embrace and turned to the windows. "Don't say that, Reed. I can't trust how I feel…not anymore."

This time he refused to let her put him off. He came up behind her. "I'm not McCarran. I'm not going to leave you." He placed his arms on her shoulders and turned her around to face him. "I care so much for you, Paige."

Her eyes widened. "Oh, Reed…"

"Don't try to come up with another argument. It won't stop the fact that whatever we had years ago is still there between us. And I still want you." He lowered his head.

He heard her breath quicken and ignored it as he captured her mouth.

Paige was weak. She couldn't resist her feelings any longer. Within the confines of his strong arms she forgot all the pain, her loneliness—everything except Reed. His tenderness reached deep inside her and nudged at her heart. His touch excited her body, making her crave him. The combination made her move closer against him.

"You make me crazy," he breathed, his voice husky with need.

She opened her eyes and looked at his face. A shiver rippled through her. Being with Reed seemed so natural and so intimate. Something she'd never shared with anyone else. She didn't want it to end.

"Good," she whispered, suddenly feeling brave as she rose up and touched her mouth to his. She may have initiated the kiss but he quickly took over. She parted for him, letting him excite her, pleasure her…love her.

His kisses were slow, and thorough, meant to drive her out of her mind. They teased her until she began to squirm. He moved his hands over her stomach, almost reverently, then continued the journey up over her rib cage and between her breasts. She soon tugged his shirt out of his jeans and slipped her hands underneath to touch his bare skin. He groaned. She whimpered as her breathing grew labored.

"Reed…"

"I want you, Paige."

"I want you, too," she confessed.

Their eyes met. His were questioning, as if to ask if she was sure.

When she nodded, he lifted her in his arms and carried her into the bedroom. The sunlight through the windows was fading, leaving the room in shadows.

Reed stood Paige beside the queen-size bed.

He watched the passion flare in her eyes. He could also feel her tremble. As much as he wanted to bury himself inside her, he didn't want her to have regrets.

"Paige. We don't have to make love. I could hold you and be happy."

Her eyes widened. "You don't want me?"

He cupped her jaw. "I've wanted you since I was fifteen years old. You've been in my dreams, in my every waking thought." He pressed his forehead against hers. "God, Paige, I can't recall a time I didn't want you."

"I've always wanted you, too," she admitted, her voice so soft, her eyes searching. "I wish we hadn't waited back then… I wanted you to be my first."

Emotions clogged Reed's throat, making it impossible for him to speak. He lowered his head and took her mouth, wanting to relay how much her words meant to him. Suddenly their need grew as did the kiss, but it wasn't enough. He wanted to finally make her his.

Reed unbuttoned her blouse and slipped it off her shoulders, then flicked the front hook of her bra, helping it off. He tore his shirt over his head and tossed it aside, then drew her back into his arms and kissed her again. He never wanted to stop. He loved the feel of her, and the taste of her.

Reed lowered Paige to the bed and looked down at her. His hungry gaze skimmed over her perfect body, then rested on the slight mound of her stomach where she carried a precious child. "You are so beautiful…" The words seemed so inadequate to how he felt about her.

He'd wanted her forever…and he was going to make sure she knew how much.

Paige blinked at the bright sunlight streaming through the window. What time was it? She raised her head and glanced at the clock. Seven-fifteen.

Relieved she hadn't overslept, she sat up as memories from last night came flooding into her head. Reed had made love to her. Her body swiftly reacted to the tender recollection. How he'd held her, stroked her through the night. She glanced at the other side of the bed to find it empty. Her hand stroked the pillow. Maybe he had to work the early shift.

Disappointed, she tried to think about her day, and all the other reasons it was best he wasn't here. That was when she heard a noise, then Reed appeared in the doorway.

"Good morning," he said.

"Good morning," she answered back.

Reed was only wearing his jeans, leaving his magnificent chest bare. Paige recalled how her fingers traced every inch of skin, and her mouth…

"You'd better stop looking at me like that, or I'll climb back into that bed with you."

She felt the excitement as he crossed the room and sat down beside her on the bed. Her gaze went to his face as she tugged the sheet higher over her nakedness. "I don't think that would be wise. We both have to go to work. In fact I should probably be in the shower." But she wasn't going to parade around in front of him.

Reed touched her cheek so she would look at him. "Paige, don't pull away from me. I promise I'm not going to push you too fast. I'm not going to move in…but please…" She watched him swallow. "Don't regret what happened between us last night."

She could see he was feeling just as insecure as she was. Besides, there were things between them that hadn't been resolved, and she was afraid that it would change how he felt about her.

"Oh, Reed, I don't regret last night. I was in

a bad space, and you were there for me… again. I was just thinking you have better things to do than to keep rescuing me."

Reed didn't like where she was going with this. "If that's how you want to explain it away, I guess I did it all wrong." He stood and grabbed his clothes from the floor. "Maybe it's time I leave." He walked out of the bedroom. While pulling on his shirt, she came after him tying her robe.

"Reed, don't leave. Please. That's not what I meant."

He slipped on his shirt. "Then explain to me what you did mean."

She just looked at him. Her hair was mussed, her makeup gone, but her brown eyes were riveted on him.

"I'm afraid, okay," she finally said. "What's happened between us has been all-consuming to say the least. And last night was so wonderful…so…"

"Incredible works for me," he coached, fighting a smile.

"That, too," she agreed. "I just don't want to confuse what I'm feeling for you with needing you."

"I don't have that problem, Paige. I know exactly what I was feeling last night."

"How can you know that? Maybe you're going on memories from ten years ago. You said yourself that I was in your dreams. Maybe you just fulfilled that fantasy."

"You're damn right I did," he told her. "But I'm not a teenager anymore. I'm a man, a man who's crazy about you." He took a step closer. "I was nuts to let you push me away before. We're meant to be together, Paige. Last night had to tell you that."

She moved into his embrace, her mouth only inches from his. "Make me believe that, Reed. Make me believe."

His mouth closed over hers as her robe separated and his hands slipped over her body. All else was forgotten.

It wasn't until evening that Paige could get her entire family together. She found she was nervous going alone. Reed had to work. Even if he were able to go with her, she knew there would be a lot of questions to answer. And she wasn't ready to do that.

She was falling back in love with him. As if she'd ever stopped. But she had a lot to deal with right now. This morning over breakfast with Reed, she'd promised to go with him to see Billy.

And that meant the truth was bound to come out. It had to. How could she move on with a relationship without telling Reed the entire story?

Paige pulled up in front of the Keenan Inn. And when she saw her parents, all problems flew out of her head. She climbed out of the car and went to greet them, along with Morgan and Leah. Holt and Corey were in the kitchen when they came inside.

"Is everything okay with the baby?" her mother asked.

"Yes, I went to the doctor yesterday to be checked out as a precaution." Paige opened her purse and pulled out her picture. "And everything is fine. I just thought you'd like to see the first picture of your granddaughter." She handed the printout to her mother.

With a unified gasp, everyone gathered around the picture.

"A girl," her mother whispered.

"I didn't know you were having an ultrasound," Morgan said.

"I didn't, either," Paige confessed. "It wasn't scheduled for two more weeks."

"How can they tell?" her father asked, squinting at the picture. "I can't see anything."

Paige went around to show them.

"Are you sure?" Corey asked. "Maybe it could be a boy."

Leah and Holt both laughed. "You know, son," Holt said. "There are advantages to being the only boy. One day you'll be happy to be surrounded by females."

"No way," the nine-year-old said.

"Well, my little girl is going to need her big cousin to look out for her."

The boy's chest puffed out. "I guess I could do that."

Paige smiled, feeling the excitement. She wished Reed was here with her. They'd spent the morning together, part of the time in bed. But then reality interrupted them and he had to go to work, with the promise to stop by later to check on her.

Morgan looked at Paige. "Where's Reed?"

Paige tried her best lawyer face. "He's probably working. Why?"

Morgan gave her a knowing look. "He just always seems to be around these days."

Paige wasn't going to be goaded by her sister. "Destiny isn't that big. Of course we're going to run into each other."

Her family were all looking at her, waiting for answers, but she didn't have any, at least, not yet.

Two days later, Reed and Paige drove out to Shady Haven. This was the first chance they both had the time off to do this. He had to get this over with—to finally put an end to the lies about his father. He couldn't move on with his life until that happened. Reed parked the truck and came around to help Paige out.

She still had her ankle wrapped, but only as a precaution. She didn't limp anymore, but Reed made sure that he slowed his pace.

They walked in and without going to the desk, he looked into the common room. There were about a dozen people, some watching television, others playing cards. He glanced toward the patio area where Billy sat in his wheelchair by the French doors. Bingo.

Reed glanced at the large male attendant, to see he was sitting off by himself. Close enough if needed, but far enough away not to hear a conversation.

"Let's do it," he told Paige.

She looked worried. "I better go first because I've visited him before."

Reed nodded, and Paige put on a smile and went to the old man. "Hello, Billy," she said.

When he looked up confused, Reed wondered if he wouldn't talk. He was wrong.

"You're that lady lawyer."

"That's right, Billy," she said. "I came to visit you before. You know my mother, Claire Keenan."

His eyes brightened. "Pretty lady. Lucky man, Tim Keenan."

"I'll tell my dad you said so." Paige grew serious. "I brought someone who wants to talk to you, Billy." She moved aside and Reed stepped forward.

"Hello, Billy. You remember me, Reed Larkin, Mick's son?"

The old man looked frightened. "No. I don't know you."

Reed didn't back off. "But you knew my father. You were his partner and helped him with Mick's Dream."

"That was a long time ago."

"Yes, it was," Reed agreed. "Almost seventeen years. That's when you said my father stole your money and disappeared, but that wasn't true, was it, Billy?"

Billy's worried gaze darted to Paige. "He wanted it all…"

"But Mick's Dream was his." Reed wasn't giving up. "You didn't like that. You wanted part of the big strike, didn't you?"

The man didn't say anything.

"What happened that night, Billy?" Reed insisted. "What happened to Mick?"

"It was an accident." Billy shook his head. "He got mad and started to fight me."

Reed's heart lurched, but he couldn't stop now. "Where's Mick, Billy?" He kept pushing. "Where is he? Tell me."

Paige touched his arm. "Calm down, Reed," she said, her voice low.

"Just tell me where Mick's body is."

"It was my fault. He just kept coming at me. I had to defend myself." Tears flooded the old man's eyes.

Reed clenched his fist. "Where is he, Billy?"

"In the mine…"

"Just what the hell are you doing?"

They both swung around to see Lyle Hutchinson.

"You have no right," Lyle argued.

"I have every right to learn the truth," Reed finished.

"There is no truth here, just ramblings of an old man."

"An old man who accused my father of stealing, and who also just admitted that Dad is buried inside Mick's Dream." He saw the worried look on Lyle's face. "This is just the beginning, Hutchinson. I'm going to find my father."

Reed started to leave and Lyle grabbed his arm.

"No court is going to take an Alzheimer's patient's word," he told Reed.

"I don't need to go to court. I'm going to search the mine."

"You can't, it isn't safe."

"Says who?" Reed asked. "Billy? I never saw a report."

"There was a cave-in," Lyle said.

Suddenly it dawned on him. "Who's to say

the cave-in wasn't man-made?" Reed asked as he glanced down at Billy. He'd already escaped into his own world. "I believe that your father has already confessed to you."

"My father isn't responsible for anything," Lyle insisted. "Besides, you can't prove it."

"Oh, I'm going to prove it, all right. So get ready, Hutchinson, because I'm about to cause another cave-in in this town."

CHAPTER NINE

DURING the following week, Paige talked with the State of Colorado division of minerals and geology, representing the Larkin family. The past two days Reed had been out at Mick's Dream with a professional crew to dig out the tunnel that had caved in seventeen years ago.

Things had started moving so fast that once they'd started the process, there hadn't been time to rethink it. The most important thing Reed had done was talk it over with his mother and sister before starting the search. Without hesitation, Sally Larkin had told her son to go ahead.

Even Lyle Hutchinson's ranting hadn't

stopped the reopening of the mine. This time his name and money had no pull. Paige made sure of that. No matter what else came out of this, she knew Reed needed to learn the truth about his father. Although she needed to prepare herself for any other truths that might come out. But she'd never be prepared to lose the man she loved again.

Tired after her long day, Paige steered her car off the highway toward Reed's house. He'd called her earlier and asked to meet him there. On the phone he'd sounded tired and defeated. As much as she'd wanted to be with Reed, he'd refused to have her or Jodi anywhere near the mine.

Paige hadn't cared to be there, either, except to give him moral support. Like he'd always been there for her. At least Holt and her father went to provide support.

The past forty-eight hours Reed was at the mine had given Paige time to think about their relationship. How close they'd become over the past few weeks.

She pulled up in front of the house, wondering how long it would last. If she and Reed were to have a future together, she had to tell him her part in sending him away.

She walked to the door, but turned at the sound of another vehicle driving up. Reed. He climbed out of the truck, and walked to her. He looked dirty and tired, but mostly he looked sad.

Her heart sank. He had news. "Reed, what happened?"

He remained silent as he continued toward her, then pulled her into his arms and held her tight. "They found a body," he said, his voice rough. "They need to run the DNA, but I know it's Dad."

"Oh, Reed. I'm so sorry." Her arms tightened and she felt him trembling as she just held him. "Have you been able to tell your mother?"

"No, not yet. I want the test to verify it's Mick, first."

She eased back and looked up at him. "What can I do?"

His dark gaze searched her face. "You're here. That's all I need."

"I wouldn't be anywhere else." She took his hand. "Come on, you need a shower and some rest." She led him to the front door and unlocked it with the key he'd given her. "Then I'm going to feed you."

They walked into the living room. She put her purse down on the side table and continued on to the hallway that led to two small bedrooms. The first one Reed had converted into an office, the second was Jodi's bedroom. Continuing down the corridor, they arrived at the master bedroom.

It was masculine with honey-brown hardwood floors, beige walls and a navy comforter on the king-size bed. On the dresser was one picture. A young Mick and Sally Larkin.

This was the first time she'd been in Reed's bedroom since the nickel tour of the house. After the morning he'd made love to her, she'd made sure to avoid the temptation. They both still had a lot to work through without continuing the physical part of the relationship. Lately they'd been focused on what had happened to Reed's father.

The funny thing was she'd been able to fall back into that comfortable space at his side. But they weren't in high school any longer, and life was a lot more complicated now. There was a lot more to lose this time.

Paige only hoped that after this was all over, Reed would take the chance and choose her.

She went into the remodeled small bathroom with the eggshell colored subway tiled shower stall. She reached in and turned on the faucet, then grabbed a big white towel from the shelf and put it on the counter. She glanced up and saw Reed leaning against the doorjamb, a half smile on his unshaven face.

"I like this. You and me together." He came inside, and pulled her against him. "I need you, Paige." He sucked in a breath. "I thought this…search would be easier… It was…hard."

"And I'm here, Reed." *I'll always be here as long as you want me*, she said silently and wrapped her arms around his waist. "We'll get through this."

He leaned down and captured her mouth. The gentle kiss quickly intensified as she opened to him and he swept inside to taste her. Suddenly he pulled back. "What was that?"

"If I have to tell you…"

"No, I mean, I felt something." He glanced down at her rounded stomach. "The baby?"

Paige smiled as her hand touched her

stomach. "I've been feeling her, too, at night mostly. You really felt her move?"

His palm pressed against her stomach. "It was faint, but it was definitely something."

The flutter happened again and his eyes widened. "It's amazing." His gaze locked with hers. "It's humbling. And in a strange way it's telling us that life goes on." Once again they were forced back into reality, and what still lay ahead.

Paige nodded as steam began to encircle them in the small bathroom. "You better get in the shower before you run out of hot water." She backed away, knowing how much he needed her, but hopping into bed right now wasn't the answer for either of them.

She walked out and closed the door. In the kitchen she punched in her mother's number.

"Keenan Inn," Claire answered.

"Mom, it's Paige. Reed needs our help."

* * *

The next day, Paige was with Reed at the sheriff's station when the news came in about his father. The skeleton they had recovered was Michael Larkin.

Reed seemed to take the news in stride, but Paige saw how much he hurt. She also saw the little boy who fought the town when everyone thought that Mick had run off. Reed never wavered over his father's innocence.

The hard part for Reed was to relay the news to his mother. Sally Larkin took the news better than expected, but both Reed and Jodi stayed close. She, too, had always believed in her husband's innocence, and though it was hard, it provided closure for her.

The day of the memorial service Paige stood outside the church with the rest of the Keenan family. She was waiting for Reed who was with his mother and sister. The van from Shady Haven arrived, followed by Reed with Jodi and little Nick.

Reed was dressed in a dark suit and tie and a snowy white shirt. He looked handsome, despite being so tired.

Paige went to him and hugged him. "Thanks for being here," he told her.

"What can I do?"

Reed Larkin had always been the strong one, always there for his family, for her…

He squeezed her hand. "Stay close by."

Paige nodded then went to Sally and hugged her. "Whatever you need, Sally, I'm here."

"Be with Reed…" Sally gripped her hand. "He loves you…"

Paige gave a nod, wanting nothing more.

Reed drew a deep breath and released it. He had to get his family through this today. He gripped the handles on his mother's wheelchair and started into the church's vestibule where his father's oak casket rested on the stand.

Reed was surprised when Tim and Holt appeared, along with his two deputies, Sam

Collins and Gary Malvern. They filed to the sides of the casket to be pallbearers.

Reed was touched. Then the priest, Father John Reilly, appeared and greeted them. He began the service with prayers and burning of incense over the casket. Then the altar boys opened the double doors of the church. Suddenly music swelled in the full chapel as a choir began to sing. The men walked the casket up the aisle and Reed and his family followed, passing so many of Destiny's residents. Reed wondered where these people had been so many years ago when his mother needed their support.

He shook away the bitterness. Today was not meant for that. Today was for his father, for what Mick Larkin stood for…for family. Reed was never more proud to be his son.

It had been a long day for Reed. After the blessing at the gravesite, people came back to a reception held at the Keenan Inn. Just an hour ago, Jodi had escorted their mother back to Shady Haven.

Since Nicky was asleep upstairs with Morgan watching over him, Reed let his sister have her way.

Reed sat on the back porch nursing a longneck bottle of beer. He was tired, but he couldn't sleep. He'd taken time off from work to recover, and to finish up the legal part of his dad's death. There still was the investigation over the cause of death, but most likely it had been accidental. That didn't get the Hutchinson family off the hook.

"Would you mind some company?"

At the sound of Paige's voice he turned and smiled. She'd been the one bright spot in all this. "I would if it were anyone else." He placed the beer down, reached for her hand and pulled her to his chair. She was still wearing her black dress, her stomach more noticeable, but she didn't seem to mind that people knew she was pregnant. "I've missed not being with you." He eased her down on his lap.

"We've both been a little busy." She wrapped her arms around his neck. "I'm hoping that's going to change soon."

He placed a soft kiss on her lips. "If I have anything to say about it, I can guarantee it." He returned for another kiss, but this time there wasn't anything gentle about his need for her.

"I want you, Paige," he whispered. "It's been too long since I've been able to hold you, touch you…make love to you."

"Oh, Reed." She kissed him. "Then take me home."

His thoughts suddenly went to his sister. He groaned. "I can't, Jodi's staying at the house tonight. I have to drive her home."

Paige smiled. "No, you don't. Jodi's upstairs with Nick. My mother talked her into not waking him up so she's staying here tonight. I guess that means I have you all to myself, but let's go to my apartment, it's closer."

"I like the sound of that."

The next morning Reed stood in Paige's kitchen. Their night together had been incredible and he wanted many more to come.

Paige needed sleep, so Reed got up to fix breakfast. When he heard the shower turn on, he knew she wasn't going to rest. At least he could help her and Sweet Pea with some nourishment to get them through her heavy work schedule.

Well, things were going to change. Paige had to take better care of herself. He was going to be around to make sure of that. He planned to be around for a long time…permanently if she'd have him.

He suddenly sensed her and turned as she came into the room. She had on black stretch pants and a white blouse. Her hair was pulled back into a ponytail and she wore no makeup. This was the way he loved her. Hell, he didn't care what she wore. He'd take her in a potato sack.

"Good morning," he greeted.

"Good morning to you, too." She walked over and slipped her arms around his waist.

Oh, yeah, he could get used to this.

"You should have wakened me," she said.

"You need your sleep. You worked hard putting together the service yesterday. Did I tell you how much I appreciated it, especially for my mother?"

"You're welcome, but Mom and Dad did most of the work. There were a lot of other people who wanted to help, too. Many of the townspeople always believed in your father's innocence."

"I discovered that yesterday. But thank you for letting me see it." He kissed the end of her nose and sat her down to eggs and bacon. "Now, you need to eat."

Paige didn't argue. She was too hungry. She'd been hungry a lot lately. "I'm going to weigh a ton by the time I deliver." She scooped up the last bite of her eggs.

Reed swallowed his bacon. "Don't worry, I'll still love you no matter how much you weigh."

Paige paused but before she could say anything, there was the sound of the bell downstairs. She ignored it but it kept up, getting more persistent. She got up from the table. "I better go see who it is. I'll be right back so we can talk."

She went down the steps and walked to the front door to find Lyle Hutchinson standing there. "The office doesn't open until nine. Come back."

He glared at her. "I need to see you now. Open the door."

Paige unlocked the door and he rushed

inside. "Look, Lyle, yesterday was a busy day. Can't we reschedule?"

"Oh, yes, the funeral for the beloved Mick Larkin. Sorry, I couldn't attend."

"I don't think you would have been welcome."

"I want to know what Reed is going to do about my father."

"I have no idea what you're talking about," Paige told him.

"I don't want the Hutchinson name dragged through the mud."

"You mean like you've done to the Larkin name for the last seventeen years?"

They both looked toward the back of the office to see Reed come out.

"Surely, *you* aren't going to try to prosecute my father."

"No, but I could sue the estate for damages. Just think, the Hutchinsons could suddenly be as poor as the Larkins were."

"That's not fair," Lyle argued.

"Not fair? Billy didn't seem to care that he took a man away from his family. Nobody thought twice that my mother had to work two jobs to support us. So why should I?"

"That's not true—Billy cared. He helped your mother keep the house. Hell, he even arranged for you to go to college."

Reed stiffened. "The hell he did. I earned a scholarship for school."

Lyle grinned. "And I have the canceled checks to show that Billy paid for four years of tuition."

Paige wanted to stop the nightmare from unfolding, but she couldn't.

"If you don't believe me just ask your girl-friend. Paige knew about it."

Paige saw his eyes begging her to say it was all a lie. To deny it. But she couldn't.

"Paige…"

"Reed, let me explain. Your mother and I only…"

His jaw clenched. "Did you help Billy get me out of town?"

"No, I just helped give you a chance at an education."

He glanced back at Lyle. "Okay, so now that you've relayed the info, you can get the hell out."

"I will, but not before you tell me what this is going to cost me. I don't want you to take retribution for something my father did years ago."

Reed stared at Paige, then looked at Lyle. "I don't want anything from you or your family. As far as I'm concerned this fight is over."

CHAPTER TEN

PAIGE told herself she had a legitimate excuse to see Reed.

For the past two days he'd ignored her calls. She wished it was because he was angry at her, but she knew that it went deeper. It was the pain she'd seen in his eyes that day in her office that would be impossible to erase from her memory.

If only he'd given her a chance to explain, maybe she could get him to understand why she'd done it. It happened a long time ago, and they'd both been hurt.

Reed hadn't known what she'd done was out of love.

Paige pulled up in front of the house next to

Reed's truck. She hadn't phoned ahead pur-
posely, knowing he wouldn't take her call.

She took a breath, got out and started up the
walk when she heard the sound of a power
saw coming from the backyard. She stepped
off the porch and went around the house to
find a large stack of lumber in the center of
the lawn. Reed was on the covered deck,
leaning over a table, cutting long strips of
wood. Not wanting to distract him, she waited
until he finished before coming any closer.

He finally turned and pinned her with a hard
gaze. "What are you doing here?"

She straightened, hiding her hurt. "I need
to talk to you, and you haven't returned any
of my calls."

"We said everything that has to be said." He
marched down the steps and followed a wide
walkway that led to a concrete slab in the
middle of the yard.

Paige refused to let him ignore her this time.

She went after him, her heels sinking in the soft soil. "This is about business, Reed." She stopped at the pile of lumber and set her briefcase on top. "The geologist's reports came back. They sent it to my office since I've been handling everything." She took out the papers, but when she looked at him, he was measuring another piece of wood and ignoring her…again.

That hurt. "Reed, give me two minutes and I'll be out of your hair."

He stood up. She saw the hard line of his jaw, his unshaven face, the dark circles under his eyes. She wanted to put her arms around him, to comfort him, but knew that he hated her for what she'd done.

"I tried to get you at the office but they said you took the week off." She eyed the concrete walkway that led to a hexagonal shaped foundation. "What are you building?"

"A gazebo. For Mom." His expression

softened. "They're going to allow her to come home for day visits."

"That's wonderful. Sally will love this."

He didn't react to her enthusiasm. "Look, I'm kind of busy. You said you had some business."

Her chest tightened painfully. She nodded, trying to get her emotions under control. "Yes, it seems that Mick was right about the silver strike. The geologist found a large vein in the tunnel where your father was...buried."

Reed took the papers and without so much as a glance, he folded them and stuck them in his back pocket. He turned away and went back to work.

His aloofness was the last straw. "You don't even want to look at the survey?"

He stood and glanced at her. "Why should I?"

"Because... Because you have a lot to think about. You could reopen the mine, work it... It's worth a lot of money."

"And it's also the place where my father died."

"I know, Reed. But as you said, Mick gave his life for Mick's Dream. You can't dismiss that." She suddenly got brave. "You shouldn't dismiss a lot of things so quickly, at least until you have a chance to know... everything."

"Some things will never heal."

"Not if we don't talk about them," she told him. "Reed, if you'll let me explain—"

"What's to explain, Paige?" he asked, glaring at her. "You lied to me. You sent me away...as if I didn't matter to you at all."

"Reed, you did matter. More than you know." She took a step closer, but he backed away. "At the time I thought I was doing the right thing, for all of us."

"You just decided to leave me out of the equation. You never gave me the opportunity to choose. Do you know what it felt like to hear you say you didn't love me anymore?"

Paige did know, because she'd felt the same pain. "We were so young, Reed. If we had tried to make a go of it…tried to work and go to school…we more than likely would have destroyed everything."

"So you just decided not to try at all. Much cleaner that way, huh, Paige?" He paced, then came back to her. "I can almost understand that reasoning, but to get hooked up with Billy…after what he'd done to my father…"

"I thought Billy wanted to help your family."

"Billy wanted to help himself. He didn't want me around to dig up the truth."

She swiped at a tear. "I didn't know that then, Reed. I only knew that you had an opportunity for an education."

Reed could only stare at her. This wouldn't matter so much if he hadn't fallen in love with her all over again.

"At what cost, Paige? You were willing to throw us aside. I loved you. You were my friend, my only real friend, and I thought I'd lost everything."

"I'm sorry, Reed."

He couldn't let her do this again. "We're all sorry, Paige. But sometimes it isn't enough. I can't do this anymore. I'll contact another lawyer to handle any other legal matters."

She nodded, biting down on her trembling lip. "I know that it doesn't mean much now, but I'm sorry things turned out this way." She turned and walked away.

Reed felt the pain shoot through him as the familiar scene replayed before his eyes. Once again Paige was walking out of his life.

It was even worse the second time.

What Paige liked about having her own apartment was that she could be alone. Alone to reflect, alone to cry. But after a few days of being miserable she knew she couldn't live this way.

She had to make a life without Reed.

For a while Paige thought about moving back to Denver. With her connections, she could make a good life there, but both she and her child needed the support of her family. Besides, she loved having her sisters close by. She also enjoyed being her own boss, and the delicious home-cooked meals from her mother. Paige hadn't shared this much time with her sisters and parents in years.

She walked into the Inn's kitchen for the weekly family dinner to find she was the last to arrive. Leah and Holt were smiling. Why shouldn't they be happy? They were in love, and were making a life together.

"Good, you're finally here," Leah said. "We have some wonderful news." She glanced at her husband who nodded. "I'm pregnant."

Cheers filled the room as everyone hugged Leah, Paige included as her sister came to her.

Paige smiled. "That must have been some honeymoon," she teased.

"It was," Leah said with a big grin. "Just think, now our babies are going to be born just months apart."

Morgan came up to the twosome. "I'm going to be a busy aunt."

"Maybe you should think about finding yourself a man and enjoying motherhood, too," Leah suggested.

"I think playing favorite aunt is enough for me."

Paige saw a flash of something in her older sister's eyes. She knew Morgan hadn't been serious about a man since college.

"Hey, where is Reed?" Leah asked.

Paige tensed. "I have no idea. Why should he be here?"

Leah shrugged. "Well, he's been around a lot since you came back to town. I just thought that you two were together again."

"Well, we aren't. I was just helping Reed find his father." Paige fought the tears. "Whatever we had ended years ago."

Leah exchanged a glance with Morgan. "Come on, we need to talk." She tugged on Paige's arm until the three sisters were upstairs sitting on one of the beds in their old room.

"Okay, spill it," Leah insisted. "What happened? I know you two were getting close again."

Paige shook her head. "Nothing happened. Reed is concentrating on his life…and I'm working on mine." Paige found it hard to hide her feelings.

"So there hasn't been anything going on between you two? That's not the way it looked to me," Morgan stated. "I thought I saw Reed leaving your office early one morning."

"Really," Leah gasped. "Oh, I miss so much living in the country. Talk, Paige."

"Okay. Okay," Paige relented. "I thought

that Reed and I could resurrect what we had years ago. It didn't work."

"We want details," Morgan said.

Paige went on to tell them about what happened ten years ago, and how Reed learned the news from Lyle.

"Doesn't Reed know how devastated you were, too?" Morgan asked. "I remember how you cried yourself to sleep. How you almost gave up your own college scholarship because you wanted to go after him."

Her older sister got up and paced. "Surely Reed can understand that you both were just kids."

"He hates the fact that I made a deal with Billy Hutchinson."

"You didn't have a choice," Leah argued. "I'll go and talk to him."

"No," Paige called. "You can't. My life is complicated enough. I'm having another man's baby. It was only a matter of time until

Reed decided he couldn't handle that. Better now than later." She forced a smile through her tears. "But I love you both so much for wanting to help." She placed her hands on her stomach. "I think the best thing now is to concentrate on my baby. I don't seem to have such good luck with relationships."

Maybe that was because she couldn't stop loving one man. And she never would.

A knock on the door brought her out of her reverie. Her mother and father peered in. "We're sorry to disturb you girls but we need to talk to you."

"Please, come in," Morgan motioned.

Claire Keenan sent a concerned look at her husband. "Go ahead, Claire," Tim said.

"Your dad and I had planned to do this years ago, but we kept putting it off. Now that Paige and Leah are both pregnant we thought you'd be curious about your biological parents, especially for their health history."

Paige sat down on the bed between Leah and Morgan. Suddenly afraid to know any more, she reached for both her sisters' hands. "Mom, if this is too hard…"

Claire shook her head. "No. You deserve to know that your biological mother loved you very much." She looked at Morgan. "I don't know how much you remember since you were about three years old when she left you here."

Morgan shook her head. "Not much, only that she'd promised she'd come back for us one day."

"Oh, honey, I know she promised, but she couldn't come back." Claire took a breath. "Your mother's name was Eleanor Bradshaw, and she had no choice but to give you girls up. Your biological father's name was Kirk Bradshaw and he was abusive toward your mother. She tried several times to leave him but he always found her. I met Ellie when we were in college. We stayed in touch over the years. When I realized what her situation was, I told her to come here with you girls, but she was afraid he would only find her again.

"Then one day she did show up, and said Kirk had become more violent. She begged us to take you girls, saying she couldn't risk you all getting hurt. And what I gathered was that Kirk was threatening her if she didn't get rid of you children." Claire looked at Tim. "Of course we agreed, thinking Ellie would come back here, but then just about six months later we were contacted by a lawyer about adopting you. We already loved you three, so we jumped at the chance to make it official."

Leah spoke next. "Did he continue to hurt our… mother?"

"We're not sure," her mother said. "We were unable to stay in touch with Ellie. At first she'd call and ask about you girls, but it was always from a different part of the country. About eight months later their lawyer contacted us and told us that Ellie and Kirk died in an automobile accident."

Paige closed her eyes. She didn't want to hear this, but she needed to. "Who caused the accident?"

"Kirk was driving," Tim said. "Later during an autopsy it was learned that your father had a brain tumor. They believe that was what caused his erratic behavior."

Stunned by the news, the three sisters sat together grasping each other's hands, trying to give each other strength. It was Morgan who pulled her sisters up and together they went to embrace their parents. And once again Paige and her sisters felt the love and security of this family. She needed them now more than ever.

Reed wondered if he should go back to work just so he could rest. Over the past week, he'd finished the gazebo, painted it and surrounded it with colorful bedding plants. He also built wheelchair ramps for both the front and back steps.

It was ready for his mother's first visit home.

A vehicle pulled up in the driveway. It wasn't Shady Haven's van, but Holt Rawlins's truck. He watched his friend stroll across the yard, dressed in jeans and Western shirt. His lazy gait seemed odd for the one-time New Yorker, but Holt Rawlins had adapted to ranch life quickly.

"Hey, Holt," he called. "What brings you into town?"

They shook hands. "Can't a friend stop by and share some good news?"

"Sure. I could use some."

Holt grinned. "Leah's pregnant."

Reed's heart tightened in envy, but he masked it with a smile. "That's great news." He slapped his friend on the back. "Must have been some honeymoon."

"It is when you're with the right woman. I sure got lucky with Leah." Holt studied him. "I was thinking that maybe you and Paige were going to get together."

"Well, things didn't work out."

"Too bad. I thought you two seemed perfect together. Leah said you and her sister were an item in high school."

Reed didn't like where this was going. "If Paige sent you here to talk to…"

Holt raised a hand. "I think you know Paige better than that. She'd skin me alive if she knew I was even here. But you have to know her sisters are worried about her."

"Why? Is something wrong with Paige—the baby?"

Holt shook his head. "No, they're fine. I just learned a little bit about what happened between the two of you and I'm not here to judge—but as your friend."

"Then butt out."

"Can't do that. You were there for me when I was having trouble with Leah." He smiled. "Believe me, I know how those Keenan women can get to you, and turn you inside out. But they also know how to love…totally, deeply…forever."

Reed didn't need to hear anymore. He'd spent sleepless nights thinking of nothing else. "I know all that. I've known the Keenan girls a long time. I still remember my first encounter with Paige. It was in third grade. I was a skinny kid then and a perfect target for the school bullies. One in particular, Robbie Carson. He loved to go through my lunch to scavenge for any food he liked. Paige marched up and told big old Robbie to get lost or she'd report him to the principal. Then she shared her peanut butter sandwich with me. And every day after that. Finally I got some height and bulk so I could handle Robbie myself."

"She's the fighter," Holt agreed. "Leah is the adventurous one and Morgan is the mother hen of the group."

Reed didn't want to think back to those times. "That was a long time ago. Things are different now."

"Are they so different, Reed? You have an opportunity to have it all, and you're blowing it. And don't say you aren't crazy about Paige and the baby because I see it every time you look at her." Holt glared. "Sometimes pride isn't worth it. In fact, it makes for a downright lonely companion."

He checked his watch. "I've got to go. If you want to talk, I'm always around."

"Thanks, Holt."

"Just don't think about it too hard. That usually gets us in trouble. All you need to know is Paige loves you."

Reed watched Holt walk away. He wanted to believe everything that his friend had said. He wondered if he and Paige had been doomed from the start. They had so much baggage this time around, and so many secrets.

Minutes later the Shady Haven van pulled up, Jodi came out of the house and they welcomed Sally Larkin home.

Thanks to the van's lift, his mother's chair was placed on the driveway. Reed took over and wheeled her to the walkway and out back to the gazebo.

Jodi had prepared lunch outside. With Nick in his high chair, the four ate together for the first time in a long time.

"It's so good to have you home, Mom," Jodi said and turned to him. "You did such a great job on this gazebo. You should have a party out here."

"I'm not much of a party guy."

He looked at his mother. "Unless they're small family parties."

"We should invite the Keenans," Jodi said.

"They were so wonderful helping with Dad's funeral arrangements."

Little Nick started to fuss so Reed didn't have to give his sister an answer.

"It's time for your nap." Jodi carried him into the house, leaving Reed alone with his mother.

"Talk," Sally said. "To P…Paige."

His mother always liked Paige. "There's nothing to talk about."

"You're a…angry." She struggled with her speech. "Not her fault. Mine."

"It's not anyone's fault, Mom."

"Y…yes. Minc." She closed her eyes, then opened them again. "I asked…Paige to help me…t…to send you to college."

Reed frowned. "What do you mean?"

"Billy…and me…"

"Billy talked to you about college?"

She nodded and tears filled her eyes. "Yes… And I w…went to Paige. She didn't want to do it. S…she loved you."

"You asked Paige to break up with me?"

His mother glanced away. "College was the only way...out."

Reed's mind was reeling. It hadn't been Paige and Billy, but Paige helping his mother.

Jodi returned with the newspaper. "Holt phoned while I was inside and he wanted to make sure that you saw the article in the paper." She opened it to the second page, finding the letters to the editor.

"Reed, you aren't going to believe this. It's a letter from Lyle Hutchinson." She went on to read,

To the Larkin Family,

First, and foremost, the Hutchinson family wants to express our deepest condolences over the loss of your husband and father. I know that the secrets that my father, William Hutchinson, kept were the cause in the delay of discovering the accidental death of Michael.

My father has been in failing health for years, and it could have contributed to his falsely accusing Mick Larkin of stealing.

We also relinquish any and all claims to any assets from Mick's Dream. All ownership will be signed back to your family. Again my heartfelt sympathy for your loss.

Sincerely,

Lyle William Hutchinson

Jodi smiled. "Can you believe it? The high and mighty Hutchinsons are taking responsibility for Dad's death." She handed Reed another envelope. "This was in the mailbox."

He saw Paige's letterhead and opened it. Inside were the papers to Mick's Dream. On the front was a note from her, saying, "It's finally back where it belongs." She'd gotten the mine for him.

He showed it to Jodi, then to his mother.

"It's over, Mom," Reed said. "Everyone now knows that Dad was innocent."

Sally nodded and looked at her son. "C… can you f…forgive me?"

Reed hadn't realized until then how much he'd been holding on to the past. "There's nothing to forgive."

She reached for his hand. "Go to Paige… No more past…"

There would always be a past, but Reed didn't want to think about a future, without Paige. "It may be too late."

"Are you too proud to grovel?" Jodi grinned. "Women love that, along with flowers and, of course, a commitment…"

Reed's spirits lifted. Did he dare hope? "You think it will work?"

Jodi hugged him. "You use the right words, and Paige will forgive you anything."

"I'm praying for that."

The next day, Reed chased Paige all around town but couldn't seem to catch up with her. He didn't blame her for not wanting to see him. He had treated her badly. He didn't deserve to have her in his life. If she'd let him, he was going to make it up to her.

Earlier, he'd learned from Holt that the weekly family dinner was tonight. With a bouquet of pink roses in hand and a ring in his pocket, he was about to crash it. When no one answered the door, he walked inside and back to the kitchen where the Keenans were all gathered around the table. He almost lost his nerve, especially when everyone turned toward him. The room grew silent as he just stood there staring at Paige.

He hadn't seen her in days, and until that

moment he hadn't realized how much he missed her. How much he hungered for her. Her beautiful face, those whiskey eyes and honey-brown hair.

It was Mrs. Keenan who got up from the table to welcome him. "Reed, what a surprise." She smiled. "Would you care to join us? We have plenty."

He tore his gaze from Paige to look at Claire Keenan. "Thank you, Mrs. K but if it's not too much trouble, I need to speak to Paige."

Paige looked almost angry. "Reed, could we do this tomorrow…we're about to eat."

"No, Paige, I need to do it now. Alone, please."

Everyone turned to her. She continued to sit there feeling the heat rise into her cheeks. "This isn't a good time."

The family members all turned back to Reed. "I guess we could have our private discussion in front of everyone," he said.

Now, she was angry, Paige got up from the

table. How dare he walk in here and start giving orders? "You have five minutes, Larkin."

She marched out the back door and stopped at the porch railing. She heard him follow her, but she wouldn't look at him. She gazed out into the fading sunlight, hoping to find calm. "I thought we said all that needed to be said."

"I was wrong," he said in a husky voice.

"Well, get it over with." She didn't want him here. It hurt to keep rehashing all this.

"I'm sorry."

She swung around in time as he held the flowers out to her. "Fine, you're sorry. Now, leave. And I don't want your flowers."

"I don't blame you," he told her and tossed them down on the chair. "I wouldn't blame you if you never want to speak to me again. I said some pretty rotten things." His dark gaze met hers.

She tried to look away, but he had a pull on her, he always had.

"I was angry and hurt, Paige."

She folded her arms to try to stop their trembling. "I understand. And I told you I was sorry. So please, just leave me alone." She turned and blinked into the fading sunlight, praying that she wouldn't humiliate herself by crying.

Instead of hearing the door shut, she felt him behind her. "I can't, Paige," he whispered against her ear and she shivered at the tremor in his voice. "I've tried. I spent ten years away from you. I don't want to do it again."

She stopped breathing, afraid to hope, afraid that she would give him the power to hurt her again.

"I could never get you off my mind," he admitted as he gently tugged on her shoulders and turned her around to face him. "And for years I tried. When I worked at the Bureau and was partnered with Trish. I tried to love her, but you were always between us. I was never able to return her feelings. She died deserving more than I could give her." There were tears in his eyes. "See, there are things we've all done that we're not proud of."

"I'm sorry…"

He placed a finger against her lips. "No more, Paige. My mother told me she was the one who talked you into convincing me to go to college."

"We both only wanted the best for you. Billy owed your family that and more."

"You were what was best for me." He kissed her gently. "You're all I ever wanted. But you were right about one thing. We were too young."

"It hurt me, too," she admitted. "I loved you, Reed. I didn't want you to go." Her eyes filled with tears. "I thought we'd find our way back together. I wrote you, but you never answered me."

Reed remembered the letters. He'd been so angry that he couldn't even look at them. "I never opened them. When we broke up and you said you wanted to be my friend, I thought that was all it was. Just a friendly letter. So I threw it away. What did they say?"

She shook her head. "It doesn't matter."

"Please, Paige. I don't want any more secrets between us."

"I told you how much I still loved you, that I was sorry we broke up and I let you go away. I hoped we could get together during the summer."

He cursed and looked away, then back at her. "I was such a fool, then and now. Can you forgive me, Paige?"

"We all made mistakes, Reed. We can't hold a grudge. We'll be living in the same town, and I'd like to think we can be friends…"

"Friends? I want more than friendship from you, Paige. I want you, all of you." He reached and lifted her chin to make her look at him. She was so beautiful in the setting sunlight. "I want a life with you, Paige, with your baby. I love you."

Her eyes widened. "You love me, but…"

"I know I messed up, but if you'll give me a chance I'll make it up to you."

"Oh, Reed. I love you so much."

He had never heard sweeter words as he pulled her into his arms and kissed her. Gently, slowly, then it quickly turned to hungry and needy, wanting to relay to her how much she meant to him. Only that would take a lifetime to show her.

"I love you, Paige." He kissed her eyelids and worked his way down to her cheeks. "I never want be without you in my life."

"I don't, either."

Suddenly Reed realized that he hadn't asked her the most important question. He stepped back and pulled the small box from his jeans pocket, then dropped down to one knee.

Paige gasped.

He took the solitaire diamond from its slot and held it up to her. "Paige Keenan, I've loved you forever and that's going to continue for as long as we live. I've come to think of your child as our child. Will you marry me, let me adopt and help you raise Sweet Pea?"

"Oh, Reed. Yes." She let him slide the ring on, then tugged at him to stand and went into his arms. His mouth closed over hers, promising her all her dreams.

A roar of cheers broke out and they looked through the kitchen window to see the entire Keenan family peering out smiling.

Paige looked at Reed. "Are you sure you're ready for this?"

He grinned. "The family is the best part."

Her parents and sisters rushed out to congratulate them, exchanging hugs and slaps on the back. "How soon is the wedding?" Claire Keenan asked.

Paige glanced at Reed.

"Soon," he said. "I want you to be mine."

She smiled. "I've always been yours for now…and forever."

EPILOGUE

IT WAS a perfect day for a wedding in a gazebo.

Paige stood in front of the mirror in Reed's bedroom in her antique-white dress. The empire-style of silk chiffon draped softly over her slightly rounded figure, angling out as it brushed the floor. The bodice had tiny straps and was delicately embroidered with silver thread and crystal beads, as was the edge of the train. Her hair was pulled up and her veil attached under the mound of curls.

"Oh, Paige. You look absolutely beautiful," her mother said with tears in her eyes. Dressed in a teal-blue dress with a short beaded jacket, Claire Keenan looked beautiful, too.

"Not too bad for being almost six months pregnant." She didn't mind people knowing about her condition. Most everyone thought Reed was her baby's father, and he loved that.

Leah and Jodi appeared in the soft pink bridesmaids' dresses. "I'll second that," Leah said. "Wait until Reed sees you." Her sister hugged her. "I'm so happy that everything worked out."

Paige felt her own tears and blinked them away. "Stop or you'll make me cry and I'll ruin my makeup."

"It's the hormones," Leah said, blinking, too. "But it's worth it."

Paige had worried about a lot of things in the past months of her pregnancy, but now she could share things with Leah and her new sister-in-law, Jodi.

Morgan entered, wearing a long strapless dress. As the maid of honor, her gown was a brighter pink than the other girls.

"Everything is ready outside." She smiled at Paige. "And the groom is getting impatient."

"So am I." They'd waited a long time for this day. During the past two weeks Reed and Paige had talked and shared their years apart. To be given a second chance was like a miracle.

Her mother kissed her and left to be seated just as her father arrived in his dark tux. He looked so handsome.

"Oh, Paige, you are a vision." He kissed her cheek. "I don't know if I can let Reed steal you from me," he whispered.

"You'll never lose me, Dad," she whispered back. "I'll always be your little girl."

He glanced at his three daughters. "Your mother and I have thanked God every day since you've come into our lives. You all brought us such joy." He took Paige's hand. "Now it's my job to give you away."

"Reed will take good care of me."

The sisters and Jodi went out. The music swelled and her father walked her out of the house to the deck and the beautiful garden before her. The gazebo was laced with greenery and baskets of flowers hung around the frame. Wide satin ribbons were draped on either side of the rows of white chairs along the aisle, and rose petals adorned the walkway that led to her man. Reed wore a dove-gray morning coat and pin-striped trousers and his eyes were on her.

The music swelled and her father escorted her down the aisle. Then Tim Keenan kissed her cheek and gave her hand to Reed.

"I've been waiting forever for you." He smiled. "But seeing you now, it was worth it."

Paige felt the pain from their years apart disappear as the minister asked, "Who gives this woman to be wed in matrimony?"

"Isn't it time to leave, yet?" Reed asked again as he watched the people seated at the dozens of tables around the yard. Some were taking another trip back though the buffet line even though they'd already cut the cake.

He was tired of smiling and shaking hands. Wasn't it time for the honeymoon? He wanted his new bride to himself.

Paige smiled up at him. "It will be over soon. Although I might be more willing to hurry it up if you'd tell me where we're going on our honeymoon."

"Not a chance," he said, drawing her against him. "Of course, if you want to try to get it out of me, I wouldn't mind some of your special interrogation tactics."

He had wanted to take Paige somewhere exotic and private, like a deserted island, but with her pregnancy, he thought it more practical to stay closer to home and decided on Coronado Island in San Diego, California.

"Just bring your bikini."

She raised an eyebrow. "I don't think you want to see me in a bikini these days."

"Oh, yes, I do. You have no idea how beautiful and sexy you look to me, carrying our baby." He glanced down at the low cut dress and her full breasts… "Have I told you how gorgeous you look in that dress, or how much I can't wait to get you out of it?"

He watched her face flush as her throat worked nervously. "You better be ready to back up those words."

This time he was the one who was swallowing hard. They hadn't made love since the day of his dad's funeral when he thought he'd lost everything. Thank God he'd wised up enough to realize how important Paige was to him…had always been to him.

"Have I told you how much I love you and little Sweet Pea?"

She went into his arms and kissed him.

"Maybe it is time to change and say goodbye to my family."

"Don't take forever," he warned.

Paige returned to Reed's bedroom where her sister Morgan was talking on her cell phone. When she hung up, she looked panicked.

"What's wrong? The town in crisis just because you took the day off?"

"Worse. That was Justin Hilliard's secretary. He's coming to Destiny next month to look over property for a ski resort."

"Oh, Morgan, that's wonderful." Seeing the distressed look on her sister's face, she asked, "It is, isn't it?"

"No! Yes! Oh, I don't know. I never expect someone like Justin Hilliard to answer my letter, or to even think about a small investment in Destiny, but now he's coming here."

"And you're going to impress him and sell him on your idea," Paige said.

"How? I'm not used to giving presentations to the CEO of a Fortune 500 company."

"Don't worry, I'll help you prepare."

Morgan frowned. "You're going on your honeymoon, then having a baby."

"I can multitask." She grinned. "We can do this."

"You can do what?"

Paige glanced at her husband standing in the doorway. "Oh, Reed. It's wonderful. Morgan has lured a hotshot executive here who wants to invest in a ski resort."

"Hey, that's great news, Morgan."

Morgan still looked worried. "I think I'll go tell Mom and Dad."

Once the door closed, Reed pulled his new wife into his arms. "I thought I'd never get you alone." His mouth closed over hers in a heated kiss. When he finally broke away, he whispered. "That's just a sample of what's in store for my new bride."

Paige looked up at her husband. She couldn't love him more if she tried. "Are we going to make it this time, Reed?"

His eyes told her of his love. "There are no more secrets, nothing between us but a cute little bundle of joy." He touched her stomach. "I have everything I could ever want. And all I ever wanted was you…forever."

MILLS & BOON PUBLISH EIGHT LARGE PRINT TITLES A MONTH. THESE ARE THE EIGHT TITLES FOR SEPTEMBER 2007.

❧

THE BILLIONAIRE'S SCANDALOUS MARRIAGE
Emma Darcy

THE DESERT KING'S VIRGIN BRIDE
Sharon Kendrick

ARISTIDES' CONVENIENT WIFE
Jacqueline Baird

THE PREGNANCY AFFAIR
Anne Mather

THE SHERIFF'S PREGNANT WIFE
Patricia Thayer

THE PRINCE'S OUTBACK BRIDE
Marion Lennox

THE SECRET LIFE OF LADY GABRIELLA
Liz Fielding

BACK TO MR & MRS
Shirley Jump

MILLS & BOON
Pure reading pleasure

0807 Rom LP

MILLS & BOON PUBLISH EIGHT LARGE PRINT TITLES A MONTH. THESE ARE THE EIGHT TITLES FOR OCTOBER 2007.

———————— ❧ ————————

THE RUTHLESS MARRIAGE PROPOSAL
Miranda Lee

BOUGHT FOR THE GREEK'S BED
Julia James

THE GREEK TYCOON'S VIRGIN MISTRESS
Chantelle Shaw

THE SICILIAN'S RED-HOT REVENGE
Kate Walker

A MOTHER FOR THE TYCOON'S CHILD
Patricia Thayer

THE BOSS AND HIS SECRETARY
Jessica Steele

BILLIONAIRE ON HER DOORSTEP
Ally Blake

MARRIED BY MORNING
Shirley Jump

MILLS & BOON
Pure reading pleasure

0907 R